Viral

Also by Emily Mitchell

The Last Summer of the World

Viral

STORIES

Emily Mitchell

W. W. Norton & Company
New York • London

Mitchell

Printed in the United States of America
First Edition

For information about special discounts for bulk purchases, please contact W. W. Norton Special Sales at specialsales@wwnorton.com or 800-233-4830

Manufacturing by Courier Westford
Book design by Charlotte Staub
Production manager: Louise Mattarelliano

Library of Congress Cataloging-in-Publication Data

Mitchell, Emily.
Viral : stories / Emily Mitchell. — First edition.
pages ; cm
ISBN 978-0-393-35053-1 (pbk.)
I. Title.
PS3613.I854V57 2015
813'.6—dc23

2015008902

W. W. Norton & Company, Inc.
500 Fifth Avenue, New York, N.Y. 10110
www.wwnorton.com

W. W. Norton & Company Ltd.
Castle House, 75/76 Wells Street, London W1T 3QT

1 2 3 4 5 6 7 8 9 0

For my parents

Contents

Acknowledgments

A number of these stories were published in magazines and journals prior to their inclusion in this collection. "Biographies" first appeared under the title "Biography" in *Alaska Quarterly Review,* where "Guided Meditation" also appeared. *Harper's* published "If You Cannot Go to Sleep," and *New England Review* published "On Friendship," "Lucille's House," and "Three Marriages." "States" appeared in *Ploughshares.*

Viral

Smile Report

Cashier #43 was not smiling enough. I called her into my office.

"But, Mr. Pruffer, I was smiling," she said. "I really was. Whenever a customer came up to my register, I smiled just like the manual says to do. I showed my teeth and everything. I lifted the corners of my mouth."

"That's not what the facial expression cognition software is telling us," I said. "The reports have been very clear for several days. Over the course of the twenty-seven documented Customer Interface Junctures it rates your facial expression at a median of five out of ten, which is really somewhere between a wan look of apology and a grimace, rather than a smile. That is extremely sub par."

Her name was Gladys Kemp. She stood in the middle of the floor in front of my desk, silent, her eyes cast down, her lips pursed as though she were holding something inside her mouth that kept trying to escape. She looked like she was in her mid-thirties. She had the first faint tracings of lines around her eyes, the blue shadows of tiredness beneath, but these things somehow only called attention to the melancholy prettiness of her face. She still wasn't saying anything.

"Look," I said, trying to project a gentler, more sympathetic attitude. "Let me show you how it works." I gestured toward the chair across from mine, and when she'd seated herself in it I turned the screen on my desk toward her so that it was at a ninety-degree angle from both of us. I leaned forward a little so that I could look more closely at what it showed. She leaned forward, too. Our faces were quite close together and I could smell something faint and lovely, lavender or green tea.

I pointed to the screen with my pen.

"The software graphs your smile over the course of the day according to a series of standardized characteristics. Broadness is only one of them. As you learned in your employee orientation, when a customer approaches it is important to raise the corners of your mouth like so"—I demonstrated for her—"so that your teeth become visible, but not your tongue. It is important to narrow your eyes and lower your lids"—again, I showed her how it was done correctly—"because the relaxation of the eye is another demonstration of a genuine pleasure experience and the customer will be able to discern immediately, if your eyes are too wide, say, or too rigid, that the smile is only a facade and not an expression of authentic good feeling. It is also important that you allow the smile to grow and fade on your face smoothly. A real smile isn't slapped on like a sticker; it blooms like a flower; it opens and closes gracefully. Like this." I showed her. Open. Close.

"I see," she said. She looked down and I saw her lips crumple laterally and she put her hand up to cover her mouth. She was still leaning forward, and now she crossed her legs, one over the other. Her straight, dark hair fell forward and she brushed it back with her hand.

"As you also should have learned when you were hired," I said, "the best way to create this expression convincingly is to cultivate the emotion that traditionally underlies it. That is, think a happy thought that might bring on a smile of its own accord when a customer approaches. Now, you have a college degree, I remember from your file."

"I have a master's degree," she said, "in biochemistry. I was going for my PhD but when the government stopped giving student loans, I couldn't manage the expense."

"Well, someone as clever as you should be able to think up something that can help you to smile at customers. I mean, really . . ." I put my head on one side and pursed my lips and raised my eyebrows quizzically so that she could see that I was addressing her as an equal, a Partner-in-Success, in whom I was disappointed and from whom I expected better work, more commitment, less slacking in the future. "Am I right?" I asked.

She was silent for a moment.

"Yes," she said, quietly.

"Of course I am. Now, what can you think of to be happy about? Let's brainstorm together about this."

She was staring downward again, and I saw that her jaw was clenched and her eyes were wide and then, suddenly, bright. She blinked a couple of times.

"Come on," I said. "Help me out here. Things in your life to be happy about."

She looked at me and blinked several more times, and I noticed that her eyes were a lovely and unusual shade of hazel brown; they seemed almost translucent, suffused all through with light. I stared into them, I admit, a little captivated, and abruptly, right there, in the chair in my office, Gladys Kemp began to cry. Tears rose and dropped from her eyes. She made a noise like something feathered being strangled and covered her face with her hands.

I let her cry for a minute before I stopped her. It's good to get the emotions out, experts say, so I handed her the box of Kleenex on my desk. Then I sat with my arms folded and watched her. She took a Kleenex and wiped her eyes with it and blew her nose.

"I'm sorry," she said, between sobs. "It's been such an awful week. My landlord is going to evict me and my daughter from our apartment for nonpayment of rent and my daughter is sick but the doctor doesn't know what's wrong and they are going to do more tests but the tests are so expensive and then our cat got run over by a bus. I've been trying to smile, really I have, but it's just been kind of difficult this month.

"I promise that I'll do better next week. Please. I can't afford to lose this job."

And she looked at me again with those enormous eyes and I thought for an instant that I might disappear inside them and become trapped the way some insects become trapped in amber and you see them stuck there millions of years later and all at once I understood that those insects weren't struggling and fighting to get out. They were luxuriating; they were deliriously happy. They were drowning in honey.

I was summoned back from these thoughts by the tune my computer plays when a new message arrives in my inbox. I was still at my desk and Gladys Kemp was watching me, waiting for me to speak. I hoped that I hadn't given any external indication of my thoughts, any sign of what I had just been feeling when I gazed into her eyes a few moments before. But her expression was unreadable: she just watched me, neutral and expectant. What would I say?

"Well," I said. "There were extenuating circumstances, I guess. As long as your rating improves next week, we don't have to make a big deal out of this."

"Oh, thank you," she said. "Thank you so much."

I nodded calmly but I didn't reply. It's best to maintain a benevolent detachment from the staff and I didn't want her to think that she'd gotten away with anything. I stood up to show our interview was over, and she stood up and she seemed relieved and excited and, before she left, she leaned across the desk and offered her hand for me to shake and I took it and she squeezed my fingers and—she smiled.

It wasn't the smile we were looking for, not the with-teeth smile of magnanimous welcome, not the one for customers. It was different from that. It unfolded diagonally across her face, her lips pushed together on one side so that the whole expression was lopsided. But it was at least a smile. A real one.

I could tell it was real because I found that I was smiling back. I was smiling as she turned away from me and walked toward the door. I was still smiling as she opened the door and stepped through it without looking back. I was even smiling as the door closed and I sat down at my computer to look at the new message that had arrived, and as I slid the cursor across the screen to open up the window for my email, and as I looked and saw that the new message was from my supervisor, Dr. Kyler, whose office is several floors above mine.

When I read the message, however, I stopped smiling.

Dr. Kyler wanted to see me. On a matter connected with standards of personal comportment. My personal comportment. She suggested I come as soon as my current Team-Member Interface Juncture was adjourned.

My Team-Member Interface Juncture was already adjourned. I took the elevator up several floors. I could see myself reflected in the metal surface of the door, but the image was warped so it looked as though my face was oozing off one side of my head. The doors slid open and I stepped out into the long, carpeted hallway and passed by the name-plated doors of the vice presidents and the directors, whose ranks I hope that someday I will join although, if I was being called up here because my conduct was not in line with the standards of the company, what hope did I have of ever having my own office on this floor? I had thought that I was doing well, managing my present responsibilities quite productively when clearly something had been going very wrong.

Thinking these kinds of negative thoughts, I arrived at Dr. Kyler's suite and knocked. Her personal assistant opened the door. He smiled at me broadly, in just the way we train all our Team Members to do, but at the very same time he also somehow managed to look me up and down with a mixture of distain and suspicion, or else a mixture of dislike and regret, or else a mixture of sympathy and contempt. I wasn't sure exactly which, but I didn't like it any way.

"She said you should just go on in," the personal assistant said and pointed to Dr. Kyler's office door.

She was sitting at her desk, putting on her glasses so she could study a sheaf of printouts that lay in front of her. When I entered, she glanced up at me—and then she smiled. Until that moment I had thought I was pretty good at generating a spontaneous expression of warmth and welcome on my face. But whatever ability I possessed paled next to the astonishing skill of Dr. Kyler. The smile that she turned on me made me feel like I had come home after a long journey, like the world was a safe and wonderful place if only I would learn to see it that way.

"Well," she said, beaming luminously. "Well."

"I came as soon as I got the message." I wanted to show her that I really cared about being a part of our company, that I was more than just an average Team Member.

"Yes. I see that and I appreciate it very much. Why don't you have a seat?" I did as she instructed. She studied the papers further. Neither of us spoke. At last, I said:

"What is it that you want to see me about?"

"Nothing serious, I'm sure," she said. "I'm sure this whole meeting is entirely unnecessary. That it is overkill. But I've always felt that it is better to nip things in the bud. Catch them before they get out of hand. I'm sure you'll agree with me."

"Of course," I said. I waited for her to continue. She cleared her throat.

"This company considers it to be of the utmost importance that our Team Members, even our senior Team Members such as you, maintain a demeanor at all times that matches with our brand. Since we trademarked the expression "Service with a Smile" all those years ago, we want to make sure that everybody, at all levels of the organization, reflects that crucial concept." She was looking intently into my face as she spoke. She was still smiling at me, of course, but now her smile had shifted so that it was less bright and more gentle and enveloping, more compassionate and caring and even slightly melancholy, as if her heart was full almost to bursting. She said: "With the Team Members you supervise, you have to be aware that they will take their cues from you. If you do not create a positive environment, they will not either.

"The facial expression cognition software," she said, removing her glasses, "tells us you have not been smiling enough. In fact, when you have been talking to other Team Members you have been looking, well . . . in some cases you have been looking what can only be described as miserable." She looked at me again. Now her smile said: *Go on and explain. Don't be afraid. You have my attention and, what's more, you have my sympathy.*

I sat there looking back at her. I opened my mouth to speak but no words were waiting inside it, so I shut it again. I thought about Gladys Kemp and how when she was telling me about her sick daughter and her run-over cat, I had stopped thinking about my expression altogether because I was listening to what she said. I felt unhappy for her and even a little—could this be right?—angry on her behalf that she had wanted to continue with her studies but couldn't do it because she did not have the money. I thought back through the preceding week and the week before and I realized that I'd talked with several of the Team Members I supervised about their Smile Reports. Each one of them had told me the reason why they weren't smiling enough: one had a husband who had lost his job and now, instead of looking for a new job, just sat at home all day watching television and drinking black Sambuca ; another had lost all her savings in a pyramid scheme based on selling nutritional supplements; another had a son who ran away from home and could not be found. When I had listened to these stories, and in fact for many hours afterward, I had struggled to generate even the most rudimentary outline of a smile. I had thought that these intervals of despondency had gone unnoticed. But obviously I had been wrong.

Dr. Kyler was still looking at me, with that expression of attentive compassion on her face. It was an expression that said: *Trust me. Let's work together to alleviate this problem.* And in response to it I promised myself silently that, beginning today, I would strive to cultivate this very look for myself. I would memorize it; I would stand in front of my mirror and practice until I got it right. I would begin right now. If she could manage to maintain her positive outlook even through this regrettable conversation, I could do the same. I took a deep breath and concentrated hard. At last I felt the corners of my mouth begin to rise.

"I apologize," I said, "for these unfortunate lapses in my professionalism. It won't happen again." Dr. Kyler nodded, encouragingly. "I hope that we can overlook them provided my future performance shows improvement."

"Oh, nothing would please me more," she said. "I'm sure that will be possible."

"Thank you," I said. Again she nodded. Then she stood up.

"Well, I feel that this has been a most productive meeting," she said.

"Yes. Well. Great. Thank you for taking the time . . ."

"Don't mention it," she said and led me to the door and let me out.

I smiled at the personal assistant as I passed his desk. I smiled at myself in the elevator going back down to my desk, although my reflection was stretched and distended so my lips looked like long pink tentacles extending from my face and undulating in an undersea current and I couldn't tell whether I looked happy or just demented.

That night, at home, in front of my bathroom mirror, while the microwave in the kitchen of my apartment thawed and then heated my supper (chicken à l'orange; mixed vegetables), I practiced pushing the lines of my mouth into a series of expressions that ran from mild amusement through sympathetic encouragement to amazed delight. I was pleased with them. I felt I was developing a skill set that would serve me well in the future. While I ate, spooning the cubes of whitish meat from the plastic tray into my mouth, I made a mental list of things that would elicit those expressions. I checked my phone for messages and found that there were none. I watched a television program about the recent, rapid growth of deserts all over the world, an unexplained phenomenon. For some reason the sand is creeping into places where it's never been before. It isn't following the normal patterns of soil erosion previously documented by geographers. Instead, it's gulping down whole towns in single afternoons, as though it was a ravening animal. A man talked to the camera about how he saw a schoolhouse in his village eaten by a wave of sand. *The ground opened like the jaws of a snake,* he said. *And then the school was gone.*

I switched off the television. I went to bed. I tried to smile into the dark but I kept thinking about the ground opening up and swallowing the building where I lived, so I found it difficult.

The next morning on my way to work I practiced my new repertoire of smiles. I felt pleased, like I had been given a second chance against the odds. But when I arrived at my office, on my desk I found a note that had not been there when I left. I picked it up and read it. It was from Gladys Kemp.

It said: *I know that this is not really usually done at work, but I wanted to thank you again for understanding about my situation and I wondered if you would like to maybe sometime meet up for a cup of coffee or something like that . . . anyway: here's my phone number.* And there was her number, all those lovely digits in a row, and I looked at them and felt the expression on my face turn serious. I felt a kind of nervous anticipation, a fluttering inside my chest. It was not a bad feeling but it made it difficult for me to maintain the sense of placid optimism that I had been carefully cultivating since I woke. I put the piece of paper face down on my desk and looked at it. I wanted very much to call the number, but immediately I thought about what might happen if I did. What if we went out for coffee and it turned out that I bored her or we did not have that much in common? What if we dated for a while and then things did not work out and we had to see each other at work every day and now it was not a happy sight but a painful one? What if we went out and fell deeply in love and I began to feel her feelings along with her, which is what should happen when you love someone very much, and I began to worry about her daughter's illness and her lack of opportunity and even her lost cat? Any of these outcomes would wreck my Smile Report. And what about Gladys Kemp? She was already struggling to keep her face under control. How on earth would she cope with any more disruptions in her life?

I swallowed hard and tried to think of calm, benign things like flowers and nice, melodic music, and with some concentration I was able to neutralize the breach in my demeanor. I stood struggling mightily and it occurred to me that if this woman had such an adverse effect on me simply by giving me her phone number, what would happen if I actually called her number and took her up on the offer to meet for coffee? It could have far-reaching negative repercussions for my entire career.

No, I thought, I can't allow that. I picked up the piece of paper and bravely, with purpose, barely thinking at all about amber light or melancholy or lopsided smiles or dark, smooth hair swept back or legs crossed or lavender or green tea, I dropped the note into the trash beneath my desk. I watched it fall among the other papers. I watched it settle. There. I had made a sound and sensible decision, one I could feel positive about. I could feel proud of myself for doing the right thing. I felt the smile return to my face and settle there, roost there, like it had come home.

Now I was ready to get to work.

On Friendship

PHONE CALLS

The reason we are no longer friends is simple, really. When I would call her last year, which admittedly I didn't do very often, she did not sound happy. Her voice on the other end of the line would be flat and uninflected, not lively and pleased to hear from me like certain of my other friends' voices when I called them. *Hi,* she'd say. Not: *Hey! How are you doing? Nice to hear from you!* Just: *Hi.* Then she'd stop talking and wait for me to continue, to step in and carry on the conversation. It was as though there was something she was expecting me to say, some problem that

I ought to know about, something I had done wrong for which I should apologize.

I did know, at least I thought I knew, what was wrong. It was that I hadn't called more recently, that I didn't call more often. For several years, there had been an imbalance in our friendship that we both felt but did not talk about. She felt, at least I think she felt, that I did not call enough, did not make enough time for her, that I held her at a distance. I felt that she expected me to call too often, that she wanted too much from me as a friend and that she didn't appreciate the attention and time I did give her.

A year or so before, she'd been going through a difficult time, a run of misfortune and disruptions that seemed to build on each other: there were problems at her job, which made her depressed and then, in part because of the depression, her partner left and then because her partner left, she decided to quit the job she disliked so much but then she couldn't find another one right away. She was the kind of person who would pick up the phone immediately if something in her life went wrong, to talk, to share her distress. She would call me, sometimes late at night, and we would talk, sometimes for a long time, about the difficult things that were happening to her. And each time we would talk in this way, I would feel like I'd paid into an account, fulfilled a requirement, and that now she could not accuse me of neglecting her. Because I am—I've always felt I am—a person who keeps her distance from people, who doesn't return phone calls right away and who doesn't like to see people too often in case I run out of things to say to them.

On the other hand she would feel—or so I can infer

from her behavior—that with each of these conversations we were getting closer and more intimate, becoming better friends. And so she began call more frequently, to talk about what was happening in her life, to get advice, to find out how I was doing. But even though her phone calls were more frequent, I was still returning them at the same rate, with the same couple-of-days delay. Only now it seemed like I was returning them more slowly, like I was pulling away from her, retreating, even though in fact my behavior hadn't changed. She made more phone calls than I returned whereas before she had made fewer phone calls and I returned a higher percentage of them. After a while she came to resent the fact that she was calling me more often than I was calling her and her voice, when we did speak, took on that flat, resentful tone that came to characterize it during the last months of our friendship.

As I said, we never talked about this. But last year, when things were going very badly with me—I was separated from my husband for a while and my new job was not all that I hoped it would be—I would think periodically that I really should call her, that it had been too long since we'd spoken, and I would sometimes get as far as starting to dial her number. But then I would anticipate how she'd sound when she answered, and the prospect of hearing her lack of enthusiasm or pleasure, of encountering yet another person that day to whom I was a problem or a matter of indifference, would stop me; I would hang up the phone and I wouldn't call.

In the end, it had been so long since I had called that I thought if I called her, we would have a fight because I hadn't called sooner and she was angry at me for that, or because I was now angry at her because I *knew* that she was angry at me for not having called sooner and what right did she have to be angry at me about a situation that was as much her fault as mine? It wasn't as if we were family, whom you are supposed to call whether you feel like it or not. What did we really have tying us together apart from the simple pleasure of hearing each other's voice on the line? And if she could not even muster that, well, what was the point of trying to stay in touch?

So I left it alone and didn't call. And now it's been a year and a half since we last spoke.

FACEBOOK

I have 143 friends on Facebook. My sister has 341 friends. I'm not surprised that she has more friends than me because she's always been the more outgoing and sociable one. She was the vivacious extroverted sibling and I was the bookish introverted sibling, because in families siblings always define themselves against each other, trying to be as different as possible so that we can figure out who we are. Hence, she has more people whom she can call friends than I do.

On the other hand, my sister isn't more than twice as friendly as I am. I would say that she's maybe 20 percent friendlier than me, maybe as much as 30 percent more fun overall. I can be aloof and difficult to reach out to; I tend to simmer and withdraw into myself when I'm upset; I can sometimes make harsh judgments about people too quickly or because I feel threatened by someone's behavior or personality or way of talking. But my sister can be explosive.

She gets into fights and tells people what she really thinks of them, no holds barred, no punches pulled. She breaks off friendships abruptly, dramatically, while I let them wither through studied inattention.

So really, those things should balance each other out and we should have about the same number of friends or maybe she should have a few more than me. But not twice as many.

I put the disparity down to the fact that I'm a person who has high standards for friendship. I don't count just anyone as a friend. For example, I don't pretend that I'm friends with someone whom I just spent time around getting stoned in college. I don't count as a friend someone with whom I just share mutual friends and acquaintances. I don't know if my sister has these high standards.

Or maybe the difference in numbers is partly explained by the fact that some of those friendships are people whom she's going to get mad at and break things off with, but that hasn't happened yet and so they are still on the rolls right now, the way dead voters sometimes remain on the list long after they're deceased. Once my sister and each of those friends have their fight, then they'll disappear because you can't stay friends with someone after a huge, disastrous fight, whereas it's easy just to have people hang around when you've just kind of let things slide between you through a gradual diminishing of contact and affection.

WAR

We were friends until the buildup to the Iraq war. We'd been friends since college and back then we were very close, him and me and whoever I was dating at the time and whoever he was dating at the time. We lived in England at the same time, right after college, so we saw each other a lot during those early, uncertain years when we were all still finding our directions in life, deciding who we were going to be and staying out late every night. And then later we lived in New York at the same time. That was where things went wrong.

When preparations for the war began, we still agreed about a lot of things. For example we agreed that the terrorist attacks of 9/11 were a disaster of terrible proportions that nothing could excuse or mitigate. We agreed that while a certain radical element of fundamentalist Islam was pernicious, it was important to differentiate between the vast majority of Muslim people, who might not agree with the West about everything and might even dislike the United States, but should not be confused with their militant coreligionists any more than we ourselves should be confused with Pat Robertson. We agreed that Saddam Hussein was a horrible dictator. But beyond that we did not agree.

I thought that the terrible events of the preceding years had showed that, in spite of all our flaws, the United States and those countries known collectively as "the West" were nevertheless better than our enemies and we should therefore try to spread our ideals, imperfectly realized as they are at home, to other countries that didn't have them yet. I thought that we had been too strategic, prioritizing security over justice, supporting any foreign leader who could keep order at whatever cost. What had that achieved, except to make people around the world hate us?

He thought that these same events showed that the

United States and "the West" had already caused too much resentment by trying to spread our ideals and that if we'd only stop trying to make everyone behave like us and acting like we knew best and imposing our version of free-market capitalism on everyone through the mechanisms of the IMF and the World Bank, people from other parts of the world might not hate us so much. Even if we could agree that democracy was a good thing, using the military to spread it wasn't just wrong, it was also antidemocratic.

I thought that Saddam Hussein was so bad that even though usually it's not a good idea to invade other countries that haven't attacked you, it would be better to get rid of him while we had the chance. He thought that sending troops into a country that hadn't attacked us, however bad their government might be, was categorically wrong. He also thought that the reasons the government was giving for why it wanted to do this—WMDs, collaboration with al-Qaeda—were bogus, a cover story that the men and women pushing it didn't even believe. I thought that, though perhaps this was so, our motives didn't need to be 100 percent pure to do some good; if we did the right thing for the wrong reasons that would be all right.

In principle we agreed that it was fine for us to disagree as long as we respected each other's reasons for thinking as we did. The problem was that after a little while, every conversation that we had seemed to circle back to this topic whether we meant it to or not. We would go out to the movies and if we saw an American film, he would always be sure to mention how it exemplified our militarism, our belief in ourselves as exceptional, our simple-minded concept of heroism through blind faith and physical exertion. If we talked about the news as it was reported abroad, I always made sure to note the knee-jerk way that America was portrayed as stupid, boorish and brutal. If we went out to a restaurant, if we discussed a book we'd read, if we related an encounter between ourselves and a stranger, everything seemed to come back to this question: good or bad? Are we (Americans) basically good or basically bad, basically better or basically worse than other groups of people? In the end it became difficult for us to speak about anything, and around that time he moved to Holland. We call each other occasionally but not as often as I wish we did now that some time has passed and those concerns, which seemed so urgent at the time, don't seem that way to me anymore.

What I remember most vividly, when I think of him, is none of that. It is a trip we took together in March just before we graduated from college. We went to France, where it was already spring, coming from New England where it was still cold and dark and snowbound. I remember that we took the train into the city from De Gaulle and emerged from the Metro into the Jardin du Luxembourg, into sunshine and green. I remember that we put our backpacks down on the grass and ran around in circles, waving our arms and laughing madly from the pure pleasure of being together in a place that beautiful.

THE GROUP

When we lived in New York, my husband, who was then my boyfriend, had a group of friends I didn't get along with. What was wrong with them? Nothing was wrong with them. As individuals, I liked them all, more or less; at least I didn't have a problem with any of them. One of them was a gifted composer; another was a well-read student of politics and philosophy; yet another was an interesting, funny and insightful writer about art and literature. But when they were all together, I found them difficult to deal with.

They were very close-knit, had been to the same college and after that they all lived in an old, converted warehouse in Brooklyn where some of them, the ones who were visual artists, had studios. They always spent time together in a big group and they liked to give one another nicknames that the whole crowd would adopt and use whether the person liked the name or not. They liked to go drinking and dancing and talking late into the night, having long, involved arguments about art and politics, making plans, starting projects. Sometimes, when they'd all stayed out too late or drunk too much, they would have disagreements that devolved into shouting and tears and people storming out and vowing never to speak to each other again. But then, like the members of a big, rowdy, extended family, they would usually make up and be friends again before too long—so even that was not really so bad.

But what really upset me about them was how content they seemed being friends with and talking to one another. They weren't always trying to find new and better friends, like most people I had met in that city. When they had a party, all of them attended and they didn't worry about whether there were other, better parties happening somewhere else to which they hadn't been invited. When they argued about ideas, they did so freely and without any apparent sense that other people somewhere else might be more qualified than they to make judgments about the subjects they were discussing. What egotism, I would think, that they believe the things they are doing and saying are actually interesting and possibly original and that they expect these things to be of interest to others besides themselves. Whereas I spend so much time worrying if anyone will ever care about what I do and what I write, and feeling that the bright center of the world is always elsewhere, that wherever I go chasing after it, it departs just before I can get to it.

So I found reasons to stay away from the group, even when my boyfriend (now my husband) would stay out late with them. It caused some problems between us because he would spend time with them and I didn't want to. In the end, we moved away from New York and that solved that problem. In our new city we didn't know anyone and so we spent most of our free time with each other and that's when we decided to get married.

KISS

Our friendship came to an end after he tried to kiss me. It was after we'd been drinking at a bar one evening—we used to like to do that, sit in a corner booth at one particular bar on 17th Street in San Francisco and talk for many hours together just the two of us. Sometimes we would invite other people along, too, my boyfriend, who I lived with, or a girl he was dating. But mostly we liked it best when it was just the two of us. We talked like people who were younger than we were at the time; we were in our thirties already, but we talked like we were still in college, all that enthusiasm, the wonderful, wandering hours of talk about all things, love and books and music and politics. I talked so well when I talked to him; it really felt like we might discover something new.

Looking back, I guess I'd always known that underneath the surface of our friendship was attraction, unacknowledged. It was in the way we looked at each other, in the time we reserved for each other; the beautiful way we spoke together was part of it, too. I guess I shouldn't have been surprised when, one day, as we were leaving our bar to go home, he put his arm around my waist and leaned in toward me, bringing his face down very close to mine before I pushed him away. I remember how his arm felt around my body and how his breath smelled of the whiskey we'd been drinking, not bad just sweet and warm. After I'd put my arms up and shaken him off, he took a step back, embarrassed, and said:

Sorry.

That's okay, I said. *I know how you feel. I do. But I live with Greg.*

Sure, he said. *I know.* Then again: *Sorry. I'd better go.*

So he went home and so did I and later that night I sent him a message saying that we could continue to be friends only if something like that never happened again. He wrote back and said okay. He said he was embarrassed by what he'd done, that it hadn't really meant anything. He really thought of me as a friend and not romantically at all and he'd hate to lose our friendship over something insignificant like this. I wrote back and said okay, I understood, although I felt obscurely disappointed when I read his message. We made plans to meet the following week as usual.

We did meet up and at first everything seemed all right between us, but after a while I noticed that he was making sure to sit a certain distance away from me on the bench instead of right next to me so that our legs sometimes touched, as he had always done before. I noticed that, where before our fingers had brushed when we would hand each other drinks, now he scrupulously avoided this contact by putting the glass down on the table in front of me. We still talked about the same things that we always had, but after a while I realized that I was unhappy. I didn't want him to simply agree that, fine, we were just friends. What is wrong with me, I thought, that he doesn't want to try to kiss me again? What was I lacking that he "didn't think of me romantically"? Wasn't I pretty enough? Wasn't I interesting enough?

Our conversation slowed and we found ourselves sitting there in silence. He tried to restart it a few times, suggesting topics that fizzled after a few sentences. I thought how I'd never noticed how much he liked to talk about himself. I thought how I'd never liked the way he talked about books as though it was a competition to see who'd read the most. I saw him looking at a girl across the room, a girl with black hair and a swirly tattoo showing in the small of her back where her tank top was riding up above her jeans. In the end we said goodbye and he didn't even try to hug me and I thought: *Am I that repulsive?* He just waved goodbye and walked away down the street.

RECIPES

For a long time, I thought of her as someone who had let me down. Some years ago, I had been seeing a man to whom she had introduced me and the affair went badly wrong. He drank too much and didn't really want to stop, and in the end I got tired of dealing with the Jekyll-and-Hyde roller coaster of dating a drunk and I broke it off. I was very sad after that because I was in love with the man in spite of his bad qualities. I felt that this was a case where one person, him, was clearly at fault in our breakup, and that as a result he ought to be shunned by our mutual friends.

When she kept in touch with him and continued to see him, I was angry with her. When she continued to go out drinking with him, in spite of openly agreeing with me that he had a problem with alcohol, I felt it showed callousness and a lack of caring on her part. I was so much more upset than he was and so much more deserving of companionship, yet I was the one home by myself while she and he and others of our circle went out on the weekends. It didn't occur to me at that time that she might be struggling with her own desire for various kinds of oblivion and with the problems in her marriage, which wouldn't last beyond the following winter.

That was years ago. We've been in touch from time to time since then, but not often and not for long and always on my side with a feeling of resentment that I could banish for a while but that would inevitably come back when other things in my life were difficult or felt unfair. Then, the other day, I was looking through a box of books that I hadn't unpacked the last time I moved and I found something she had made for me when we used to live in the same city. It was a book of recipes she'd compiled, chosen by her and handwritten into a hardbound notebook complete with pasted-in pictures and hand-drawn designs to make them look nice. The notebook was full from end to end and divided like a real cookbook into sections: soups, main courses, desserts, drinks. I looked through the book and thought how I had not yet made any of the recipes it contained. I took it out of the box and put it on the shelf with my other cookbooks. I thought how much trouble had gone into making it and how I couldn't think of any time I'd taken that much trouble over something that was meant for just one other person to enjoy. I thought: I should really, really call her and tell her that I found this. So I searched until I found her most recent number, took the phone to a comfortable armchair in one corner of my living room, dialed the number and listened to the phone at the other end start to ring.

COMPANY

My oldest friend and her husband had their first baby last year. I've never been that interested in babies, really. I perceive that they are very beautiful, so beautiful it's sometimes hard to bear. But I don't want one of my own and I'm not sure why other people do. They are adorable when they smile, but when they cry it feels like having your heart removed with a pair of knitting needles and no anesthetic: you'd do anything to make it stop. And then, as well, you can't go out at night, you have no privacy, you have to be an example for someone all the time, etc.

This friend is someone I've known since we were teenagers. In high school, we were always together; we used to have private, extended jokes, some of them not very nice, about the kids at our high school who were more popular than us—which was almost everyone—and this helped us get through those difficult years and feel less miserable and insane. When we went to college, unlike many high school friends, we kept in touch and visited each other.

I've known her husband for many years as well. When we were in our twenties, there was a period where we all three shared an apartment together and we were like people who share an apartment on a television program, always talking and very involved in each other's lives.

So when my friend flew up to visit her parents in Virginia recently, I decided to drive down from Pennsylvania, where I was teaching at the time, to see her and meet her baby.

I was looking forward to the visit, but not without some reservations. I've had other friends who've had young children, though never such old, close friends, and particularly when the kids are very young you can't really sustain a conversation with the parents. There is always something that the baby needs: his diaper must be changed, or he must be fed, or he must go down for a nap, or he needs to be walked around to prevent him crying. I was thinking: okay, so we'll have a few minutes to catch up between his crying fits; that will have to do.

Actually, if I'm honest, in the past few years I'd started to feel a distance grow between my friend and me. She now has a real, grown-up job in public administration, and she and her husband have bought a beautiful, old, wood-frame house in Atlanta where they live. I am still moving around every couple of years, bouncing from job to job, still working on my stupid novel. Sometimes I feel like she's become one of those kids we used to be snarky about in high school. She's managed to make the transition into being normal and I'm still out here looking in, but now there isn't even anyone to keep me company.

Anyway, when I arrived at her parents' house, where my friend was staying, I rang the doorbell and she answered it. On her hip was her baby: a little boy with a thick silky head of black hair like hers and her husband's bright blue eyes. I looked at my friend and at her baby. There they were—my friend and her husband—mixed together into one person. Of course, in one sense, this was just what I'd been expecting; the genes of parents combine to make a child. But on another level it was a total surprise. How is that possible? It's like magic, really. The baby is both of them and neither of them. When this little boy looks serious and thoughtful, there is my friend's contemplativeness; and when he grins or laughs out loud, there is her husband's good humor.

My friend leaned around her baby to hug me with one arm. "Come in," she said. "It's so nice to see you."

I stepped into the front hall, took off my coat and hung it up. My friend's baby watched me do these very ordinary things as if they were the most fascinating spectacle he'd ever seen. He didn't even seem to blink: just looked at me in absolute amazement. And without really meaning to I stared right back at him.

My friend said: "Would you like to hold him?"

"All right," I said, uncertainly.

I stood in the hall and she passed me her baby. He was somehow heavier than I'd anticipated and he seemed to have one too many limbs so that whatever way I held him there was always an arm or leg either dangling out or squashed. After a few moments of awkward shifting around, trying to find a comfortable position for him, his face crinkled up and he started to cry.

"I don't think he likes me," I said, trying to give him back.

"Oh, no," my friend said. "Don't worry. Just try walking him around."

I walked around the entire ground floor of the house bouncing him until eventually he stopped crying. Then I sat down on the living room sofa with him on my knee. He looked at me again with that same solemn expression on his face he'd had at first. He was watching me like he had all the time in the world to do it.

My friend came and sat down on the couch beside me. "Look who's made a new friend," she said. I wasn't sure if she was talking to her baby or to me or to both of us, but I didn't answer. I just kept watching the baby, waiting to see what he'd do next.

Lucille's House

Her mania for wallpaper reaches its apotheosis inside the walk-in closet off the bedroom. Silver, with giant white outlines of magnolia flowers sketched across it. Its surface reflects, so she can see her own movements, the warmth of her arms, as she reaches up to shuffle through the racks of dresses and shirts. But it's not so smooth that the image is clear. Looking at it, she can see just enough of herself to be certain she is really there. And then for the interior of the bureau: a textured foil, also silver.

Charming, the designer says. Not many people make such bold choices, Mrs. Armstrong. But then not many people possess your impeccable, inimitable style. Lucille just looks blankly at the woman; she is pale, with a weak chin and thin blonde hair that falls lank around her face. This is not the first time the designer has embarrassed them both with her overly lavish compliments.

When the room is finished, the flowers on the interior doors don't match up with the flowers on the rest of the wall. You'll have to redo this, she tells the designer. I want the pattern to be continuous across all the surfaces.

She met Louis when she was dancing at the Cotton Club. "The Ebony Rose," she was called, the only dancer on stage whose skin was so dark that she had to wear it all the time, couldn't slip out of it to pass for Italian or Greek when that suited her better. He was there, fronting the Hot Seven with his photographer's flash smile and that voice that seemed to come from the soles of his feet, from some other, richer world. She finished her last number and came off the stage, and he was there in the wing, grinning and looking at her like he could have eaten her up in one bite if he were inclined, but, as a gentleman, he'd refrain and instead consume her slowly, piece by marvelous piece.

"Glad to see they're finally letting real women dance here," he said.

"What do you know about women that you can tell the real ones from the rest?"

"A few things." He hadn't left off smiling. "I married three just to make sure." And then he reached up and cupped her chin in his hand and ran his thumb along the arc of her cheekbone and down to her lips. She thought it was the gentlest touch she had ever felt. She shook her face free of his grasp.

"What would I want with a man who's already gone and got himself married to three other women?" she asked him. He laughed.

"Oh, no. Don't worry. At the present time, I'm only married to one of them."

He is in Chicago the following winter to play a gig, and he figures he might as well get his divorce while he is in town. He is making his statement before the judge when he glimpses Lucille sitting in the back of the courtroom. He had not expected her to be there. She is wearing a dark blue coat with a high collar and a hat of the same shade with a small feather on the side. She is trying to be inconspicuous and failing. The eyes of the men in the room swing toward her like the hand of a compass to north.

After the proceedings are finished, he comes to where she is sitting.

"What are you doing here?" he asks her.

"I'm making sure you are really getting a divorce."

"Well, I did it," he says. "You saw me." He looks at her hard. Then he offers her his arm and together they walk from the courtroom. As they are going down the steps, he glances over the balustrade and sees a line of people waiting outside an office on the ground floor. They are chattering happily—a marked contrast to everyone else in the building. It is the office that issues marriage licenses.

"Lucy," he says. "Honey." He indicates the line of waiting couples with a soft movement of his head. "Want to get married? I mean, since we are already here."

. . .

"Buy us a house," he tells her on the telephone from San Francisco.

"What kind of a house?"

"I don't know what kinds there are to choose from. Just find one you like."

The house on 107th Street in Queens is a three-story clapboard affair on a small lot. The street is quiet. Most of the residents are Irish or Italian. Their children are playing kickball in the road when the realtor ushers her up the front steps and opens the door. She follows him around the three floors inside: the bedrooms; the study, which lets out onto a balcony overlooking the street; the big basement. She likes it at once.

She looks out the backdoor into the yard. There is a single broad-trunked plain tree shedding its spiky globes of seed onto the thin winter lawn. She remembers a tree like that from the end of the street where she lived as a child. She remembers crushing the pods under her shoes . . .

"I'll take it."

"Mrs. Armstrong, are you sure you don't want to see a few more properties before you make up your mind?"

"Yes, I'm sure. This is the one I want." She doesn't tell him that she has never lived in a house of her own. Throughout her childhood, her family moved from one rented room to another to another after that. If they left before the rent was due, they called it "Beat the Rent," It was a game, like Catch the Hat or Go Fish, where winning meant you were gone before the landlord came around on the first of the month to collect. Then in New York, she lived in a ladies' rooming house: one small room, clean, easy to understand.

Looking at more houses, she thinks, would only clutter her head with too many kitchens, too many front porches and backyards and basements and staircases. She doesn't like confusion.

Louis arrives at his new house in the middle of the night. He has just come from the station, and before that from engagements in Cleveland, St. Louis, and Detroit. Lucille sends a driver to meet him because he doesn't even know the address yet. She sees the car pull up by the curb outside, sees him in the back, his trumpet case on the seat beside him within arm's reach. The rest of his luggage is in the trunk, but his trumpet he always keeps close by him when he travels. She says, you act like it's your pocketbook, the way you clutch that thing. He says, it is my pocketbook. You get money out of your pocketbook, right? Well, I get money out of this . . .

He leans forward and says something to the driver and then sits back against the seat. He doesn't get out. He remains seated where he is in the back of the car. Occasionally he shades his eyes with his hand and peers up at the house through the car's side window. What is he doing? The car is still sitting at the curb, its engine running, but he shows no sign of moving.

After a couple of minutes, she puts on the porch light and opens the door. She waves down at the car. He waves back and then climbs out and goes around to pull his cases from the trunk. The driver goes to help him, but Louis tips him and then waves him away. He comes up the steps.

"What were you waiting for?" Lucille asks when he gets to the top.

"Well, I wasn't sure this was the right address," he says. "I didn't want to go knocking on someone else's front door in the middle of the night. What would you think if some strange black man came to your door in the middle of the night in this neighborhood?"

"I would think he probably needed a cup of coffee."

"You know what I mean."

"Sure, but I gave you the correct address, baby. I can see you've got it right there." And indeed, he is holding the piece of paper she gave to the driver. It has the address written on it in her own handwriting.

"I know. But, honestly . . ." he is looking past her now into the front hall. His eyes look like a child's at Christmas before the presents are opened. "I didn't believe that a house this nice was mine. Is it?" She sees that he is crying. He has never had a house of his own before, either.

"It is," she says. "It's yours. I promise."

When they are in Paris during his European tour, a man they meet at a party insists that he wants to paint Lucille's portrait. He trails Louis around the room, conversation to conversation, explaining that his wife's is the most marvelous face he's seen in years and he must be allowed to render her likeness. Such perfect lines. Such wonderful tones. They can have the painting as a gift when it is finished.

She isn't sure she wants a big picture of herself hanging

in her house; there is something that unnerves her about the idea of her own face preserved in paint while she grows older watching it. But Louis loves the idea, and before she knows what has happened, he has arranged for the man to accompany them around Europe so she can sit for him every day. She shrugs. It will give her something to do during the long hours when he is rehearsing and performing. And when the picture is done, it can go in his study, she thinks, somewhere she won't have to see it all the time.

In Morocco, she sees a carved wooden screen in the bazaar, which she realizes would look perfect by the front windows of the living room. In Berlin, there is a vase glazed blue and gray, all hard angles and geometry, which she finds in an antique shop on Keithstrasse.

"For the shelves in the breakfast nook," she tells him, when she unwraps it on the coffee table in their hotel suite.

"Looks like you should put square flowers in that, flowers with sharp edges." He turns it around in his hands.

"Well, you find me some flowers like that to go in it," she says to him. "But in case you can't, I think ordinary round flowers would do fine."

In London, in the window of a shop on Kensington High Street, she sees a child's mobile made of wood and painted in bright primary colors. It plays a tune when it turns. She watches it through the glass for a while. He comes up beside her quietly and puts an arm around her waist.

"You want that?"

"Not for me," she says. "No, I don't want it."

"If you want it, get it. I'll go in and get it for you."

"I told you I don't want it. What on earth is the point of

having something like that . . ." She trails off, annoyed at herself for having been caught staring, annoyed with him for pressing the point. He has no children. None of his other wives ever conceived as far as she knows.

"Let's go," she says, turning away from the window full of toys. "I think I'm ready for some lunch."

That evening he brings her a dozen roses in all different colors—red, pink, white, yellow.

"Flowers with sharp edges," he says, pointing to the thorns. She smiles and puts them in the blue vase.

In Ethiopia, they are given a painting done on leather stretched over a wooden frame, of Moses receiving the commandments on Sinai. The sepia-colored figures have huge deer eyes and muscular-looking halos. They look content.

She thinks it is time to go home.

When he is away she keeps busy. She has lots of friends and acquaintances in New York. She dines out often and has her women friends over for bridge. She volunteers for the Urban League. They talk on the phone from wherever he is, out on the road. She says: Tell me what you can see out of your window. I can see the Seine, he says or, I can see the Nile. I can see Hyde Park corner. I can see that damn wall and all the barbed wire they've got to stop people getting from one side to the other. And the guard towers that they shoot people from.

She decides to renovate the kitchen. Louis will be on tour for another couple of months, so she can get most of the work done before he returns. She decides on an ocean blue for all the cabinets. She tells the designer she wants the doors to curve: no corners, just a smooth undulating front. And she wants certain things built into the counter so they disappear, folding away when she doesn't want to use them: a bread box, a can opener, cutting boards.

When the room is done, she feels like she is on board a ship whenever she steps into it, because no space is wasted, there is no clutter or inefficiency. The feeling pleases her, and for a few days she finds herself drawn into it repeatedly just to admire its clean simplicity, to run her hands over its smooth new surfaces, to inhale the fading odor of fresh paint and varnish.

Louis calls her from Amsterdam.

"I will have to do another couple of nights at the end of this. Another week or maybe two on the road. You want to come out here and join me, honey? We could go to Nice for a while when it is all done."

She shakes her head insistently no, and it is only after a moment that she realizes that of course he can't hear this gesture over the phone lines. She doesn't want to go back to Europe. She has had enough of traveling.

"You just come home as soon as you can," she says.

"I will. Just as soon as we're done recording . . ."

After they hang up, she goes down to the kitchen and opens the cabinets slowly, one after another. The next day she calls her designer in and begins picking out molded wallpaper for the front room and the hallways. Mirrored walls for the bathroom downstairs. She likes the idea that each room will have its own texture.

"If I go blind," she tells the designer, "I want to be able to tell where I am by touch."

. . .

He comes home and the house is full of people. The grown-ups sit in the living room and drink cocktails. Louis takes his little niece on his knee and teaches her how to burp on purpose until her mother makes him stop. Or some afternoons he will stand out on their upstairs balcony and play his trumpet so that the sound carries up and down the block. The neighborhood kids know that this is the signal: there will be a movie in their den that night, cowboys and Indians. There will be popcorn and soda served by Lucille. Louis runs the projector and then sits among them in the big, sagging, leather armchair in the middle of the room. Sometimes he will show a reel of cartoons before the main film, just like at a real movie theater. At the end of the evening, all the children go home and the house is quiet and empty. They make their way upstairs to bed.

From one of his trips, this one to California, he brings her a glass tumbler hand painted with sixteen positions from the *Kama Sutra*. Stick figures of a man and a woman engage in coitus from every angle that she has ever imagined, and a few she can honestly say she never has.

"What do you think?" he asks, barely able to keep a straight face as he watches for her response.

"I love it," she says, her voice flat. "I love it so much that I may have to break it so I don't have to share the privilege of seeing it with anybody else."

He puts it on the low bureau in the front hall and stands back to admire it, hands on his hips, hamming it up for her benefit.

"Oh no," she says. "Oh no. You aren't going to keep that thing there, not with all the children we got coming and going through this house all the time. No way."

"They won't know what it is. They won't even notice it. Perhaps it will work its way into their unconscious minds and help them out, you know, when they get older . . ."

"Well, that is thoughtful of you. But no way. You put that thing upstairs, somewhere out of sight."

"Okay," he says slowly, turning to look at her. "Okay. I'll make you a deal."

"What deal?"

"That picture of you, the painting that crazy French man did, the one you've got stuck away up in the study where no one but me ever gets to admire it?"

"I know the one you're talking about."

"You let me bring that down here. Hang it in the living room. Where everyone can see how beautiful you are. And then I'll move my pornographic liquor glass up to the study and put it on a back shelf where no one under the age of twenty-one is ever going to know it's there." He folds his arms across his chest, satisfied. "Deal?"

"Okay. Deal. But with one more condition."

"What is it?"

"You have to move that damn picture down here yourself if you want it on display so badly."

Sometimes a journalist or, more rarely, one of their guests (who is afterwards never ever invited back) will ask about the things that some of the younger musicians have started to say about him. It always begins the same way: People say that your music has become too popular. How do you respond to that? Or, You know, it has been said that your stage persona is too . . . friendly. Lucille particularly hates this one. What does that mean, "too friendly"? She knows what it means; she heard the comments in their original, uncut form. They say he is clownish, that his good humor lacks dignity, that it panders to white notions of what a black man should be.

Louis always fixes the person with a direct look. What do you think? he asks. The answer is usually deafening silence. He never gets angry about the questions, or not so as anyone could tell. He leaves that to Lucille.

"So let me get this straight," she says after one of these occasions. "Before it was a problem for a black man to be too serious in public, and now it's a problem for him to be too funny?"

"That seems to be the size of it," he says. They are sitting at either end of the breakfast table, drinking their morning coffee. The sun is coming through the gaps in the blinds making frets on the floor. She rises and comes over to him, taking his head in her hands and cradling it against her belly.

"How does it feel to be a problem?" she asks quietly, speaking to the air around her as much as to him. *Being a problem is a strange experience—peculiar even for one who has never been anything else . . .*

She isn't with him when he has his first collapse. He is in the studios over in Manhattan and suddenly he feels lightheaded. Hot and cold waves undulate through his body, and he sits down, abruptly, then falls. He is rushed to the hospital.

This is where she finds him, propped up in bed on a pile of white pillows looking pale but not frightened. She comes and sits beside him.

"Baby . . ."

"I'm all right," he says.

"You gave me such a scare."

"They say I need to take it easy for a while. No more touring. No more playing or recording for a while. Get some rest."

"Well, you better do what the doctor says."

"Yeah, I suppose I'd better. They say I might not be able to play like I used to." He sighs and then looks down at his hands, which are lying on top of the sheet as though they don't belong to him, as though they are something someone else left behind when they came to visit. In his face she sees, more clearly than she has in all their years of being married, a deep seam of sadness that stretches down, down, out of sight. And she knows it goes all the way through him, back to New Orleans, to Storyville, to when he was a child, to the sound of women laughing from upstairs rooms with locked doors, the sound of women crying for their lovers who've left, the smell of men getting drunk in the afternoon. She remembers those things, too, from another city but the same. Suddenly, he looks up at her, looks into her face. His eyes are wide and serious.

"I've got to show you something," he says.

"What?"

"I can't tell you. I've got to show you. You ready?"

"Yes," she says, straightening her posture. "I'm ready."

He reaches down beside the bed. There is a loud mechanical buzzing sound, and she realizes that he is slowly tilting away from her, the top half of his body moving steadily downward until, with a click and more buzzing, it begins to move back up.

"Check out this bed!" he says. "The bottom part moves, too, you know, the legs. Look." He presses a different switch and his legs begin to elevate slowly until they are nearly level with his chin. "Is that great or what? Come on. You can have a go, too." He lifts up one side of the covers and pats the mattress. She hesitates, then slips off her shoes and climbs into bed beside him, laughing while he moves the levers so the bed rises and falls beneath them.

After a while he can't manage the stairs, and she has an electric chairlift put in so he can get up to the second floor.

"Better than that bed," he says. He rides up and down in it for fun. He is restless, wanting to do more than he can handle. He records the conversations of people who visit them, the sounds of their street, sometimes. He sits in the garden when the weather is nice.

She makes food for them and they eat supper out on the patio. He is on a new diet.

"I can eat fish and rice and salad," he tells their guests. "Or I have the choice of rice and salad and fish. Or sometimes on special occasions, salad and fish and rice. But no liquor. Isn't that a terrible injustice?"

One evening, she finds him standing out on the balcony of his study upstairs. The day has been especially golden and now the light is slanting among the low buildings as the sun makes its way from the sky. He has his trumpet out of its case for the first time in some weeks. He puts it to his lips when he sees her and plays, something slow and sweet that she doesn't recognize. It must be new. She sits down at his desk and listens to him.

"I think I'm ready to get back to work," he says. "I feel good. I'm going to call up the band tomorrow." He inhales deeply, holding onto the railings and looking out at the street where they have lived for thirty years.

That night Lucille wakes up suddenly and opens her eyes in the darkness. When she listens, she cannot hear him breathing anymore.

She knows it is not a healthy impulse making her insist that the closet needs to be wallpapered all over again. She understands perfectly well that it is neither necessary nor appropriate for her to demand that the flowers match up. But she doesn't care. She is angry, she realizes after the designer leaves, politely promising that the men will come to strip and repaper the walls before the end of the week. She is angry because here she is in this house and all she has left is money. It is not that she objects to money as such. She is not sorry to have it. But by itself, it is something of a disappointment.

She papers the interior of the bureau herself, pasting and smoothing the foil into place in each of the twelve drawers, top, bottom and sides. Sometimes when she is working, she forgets that this is anything more than another temporary absence. It is not that she thinks it: once she begins thinking the game is up. But she feels, fleetingly, that he will call, from Cairo or Los Angeles or Hamburg. That he will be on his way home any day. She is going to finish fixing up the house just as though he was still there to come back to it.

But at a certain point there is nothing left to do. She walks from end to end of the place, and every inch of it is just as she envisioned. She sits down on the couch that faces the bay window in the living room and watches the street shift quietly in its bed. Sometime later, it might be hours, or months, or even years, she isn't sure, there is a ring on the doorbell. When she opens it, a young man is standing there. He asks if he can come in.

He says:

"I used to come here to watch movies sometimes. My family lived on this street but they moved away. The Harrises, Sharon and Roy. I'm sure you don't remember . . ."

But she does. "Terrence, right?" she asks.

"No," he says, "Terry is my older brother—lives in Chicago now. I'm Jake."

"That's right," she says. "You wanted to play baseball when you grew up." Terrence and Jacob. They were as alike as twins but cast from different-sized molds, she recalls, though both had these astonishing legs that stretched practically to their chins. Terrence was the noisy one, the natural performer. Jake was the reader.

"Do you ever have movies here now?" he asks, a little later, over a glass of tea. "For the kids that are around here these days?"

"I haven't done that since Mr. Armstrong got sick," she says. It hadn't occurred to her to do it without him. She can't really even imagine a room full of children without him in the middle of it.

"Well, that's too bad. Those are some of my best memories, sitting on the floor downstairs here, watching cartoons, getting my fingers all covered in butter and salt. You should think about starting that up again."

When he goes away she forgets about what he has said for a while and then, one day, it is there in her head, this idea, as though it has simply been waiting for the rainy fall weather to come back. She thinks, today is the day for a film. But she realizes that without Louis she doesn't know how to tell people what is going on. For a while she is stuck and then she has an idea.

One by one, she takes the speakers down from where they sit on the shelves of his study. Each one is encased in a solid wooden frame and they are heavy to lift. Where they have been standing on the shelf, there is an outline marked in dust, and she tuts to herself; she thought she'd kept the place neater than that. She opens the French doors and carries them carefully out onto the balcony so that they are pointing into the street. Then she goes to the cupboard where he kept all of his recordings. She realizes to her profound surprise that she has not listened to any of them since he died.

She thumbs along the spines of the eight tracks and chooses one. Something from one of the sessions he did with Ellington, she isn't sure exactly what is on there, but she has a feeling about this one. She slides it into the machine and presses "play" and listens. It is beautiful and sad, the music like a whirlpool, and within it the sound of his trumpet is a smooth, strong fish with shimmering scales along its length. It pulls her down into the depths of the song. And at the bottom of all that glorious sound, there he is. He has been here all along; when she thought she was all alone, in fact he was only waiting here for her to find him. *You didn't know?* the trumpet is saying to her now. *This song is for you. And so is the next one. And the one after that one, too.*

Is that so? she asks into the sound.

Yes, the trumpet says. *Here; listen.*

The trumpet pauses and the band plays a few chords of introduction. And then out over the street, his voice goes like a flag, like a banner, like a story of what is to come.

States

An Itinerary

NEW YORK

We at Solitary Sphere Travel suggest that you begin your visit to America with a few days in New York.

Be prepared for culture shock when you arrive. People in this city are infamous for saying what they really mean, and after the polite evasions of our own culture this may grate a little on your nerves. Try to remember that this is just the way Americans behave: they think it is a good idea to say whatever comes to mind regardless of the consequences. In New York the effects of this bluntness are even more pronounced than elsewhere because everyone has to shout just to be heard over the traffic.

New York City is not the capital of New York State, although it is the tallest city. There is some dispute about whether it is largest in terms of population, since many of its denizens have been shown conclusively to have several different lives and personalities, each of which they inhabit for part of every day. This makes them difficult to get to know on all but the most superficial level.

Regardless of this, New York City is truly a world city, replete with grand avenues, skyscrapers and beautifully maintained city parks. It contains a multitude of artistic and cultural institutions and other tourist sites. These include the famous Statue, which stands guard over the harbor, raising her reading glasses in her left hand to peruse the great book clasped in her right. What is written on the stone pages of this book has been read only by a handful of workers and restorers, as it is impossible to see either from below or from the platform on the brim of the Statue's bowler hat to which visitors can ascend by means of an interior staircase. These workers say that the pages of the book contain lists of slurs aimed at every race and ethnicity that has ever come to this most polyglot of cities, ranging from the thoroughly archaic to the most contemporary. The city fathers were not aware of this when the Statue went up (it was a gift from abroad), and by then it was too late. Periodically, a citizens' group will protest publicly that the book's contents go against the spirit of the city and should be erased, but someone else always counters that it would be wrong to destroy a famous work of art by altering it so drastically. The argument goes on until everyone gets tired or distracted by some more urgent problem. Because all groups are insulted with equal virulence in the pages of the book, no particular faction has been motivated to mount a sustained campaign to have the offending matter removed.

Make sure you see the Statue, along with the nearby Museum of Imaginary Art, world-famous for its absence of exhibits, and the zoo.

New Yorkers are brash in public, but they are gentler in their private lives. You'll find the homes of New York are frequently decorated with mirrors in unlikely places. Some people attribute this to unusually high local levels of vanity, but really it is because people in New York tend to live in small houses and apartments, and mirrors make their rooms look bigger.

Recently there have been numerous cases of haunted mirrors in New York, and this has caused problems for the police as well as for residents. A typical haunted mirror appears normal until it is hung on a wall and then the surface shifts, warps, and becomes a reflection not of the room or person physically opposite it but of the place the viewer really wishes to be. This can be a disturbing thing to learn about yourself or about your spouse, and a number of apparently happy marriages have been damaged or destroyed by haunted mirrors. The attorney who led the class-action suit against the manufacturers said in her briefing to the press: "You think that your husband is content at home, and you discover he'd rather be trapped in a factory that manufactures beads with a woman he once sat next to on an airplane. My clients and I consider that this forced disclosure of subconscious desires causes undue pain and suffering to the victims and, in many cases, significant loss of income."

The police have been instrumental in disturbing the

chain of supply for the haunted mirrors, though some residents feel they could be doing more.

The official state vermin of New York rotates biannually between the greater glowering cockroach and the egg rat, which can be distinguished by its blue webbed feet.

CAR RENTAL

Once you leave New York, we suggest you rent a car, even if you do not usually like to drive. You will find that driving in America is quite different than it is in other places in the world. In most countries, the roads are narrow, badly paved or steep. Driving requires skill, practice and concentration.

But in America, the landscape has been redesigned so people can slide through it seamlessly inside their cars. When you get behind the steering wheel, you feel as though you have finally arrived at your intended destination. In America, it is not driving that is difficult. It is finding a way to stop.

PENNSYLVANIA

Pennsylvania is the softest state in the Union. It is a good place to continue with your journey.

Early in its history, when it was still a colony, Pennsylvania passed an ordinance outlawing sharp corners for the good of the citizens. As a result, the craftsmen of Pennsylvania pioneered a style of furniture making that came to be known as "Rustic Curvature" for its solid forms and smooth, undulating lines. In recent years, reproductions of these designs have been enjoying a renewed popularity.

The no-corner rule meant that Pennsylvania never

became a center of industry like many of its neighbors but instead has remained indebted to agriculture for much of its economic base. The statute has never been removed from the books, though today it is rarely enforced.

In Pennsylvania, the mountains are shaped like breasts. This is not discussed by most people or taught in the public schools. The culture of the rural western half of the state tends to be conservative and also to exhibit a great love of birds, fried foods and small boxes. People there are friendly and belligerent at the same time, which is an unusual combination. Good friends greet each other by pretending they are going to punch the other, then drawing back at the last moment. For first-time visitors, this custom can be unnerving. If someone seems like they're about to punch you during your time in Pennsylvania do not be alarmed; it just means they consider you a friend.

Pennsylvania is an old state and therefore a sad one. More than two hundred years ago, it was vivisected so it could be made into farms. The houses peel paint, and the little towns, knotted around crossroads, seem often to have forgotten what they wanted to say next. We recommend that you stay in Pennsylvania for only a few days, even if you will be in America for several months, because after that the sadness can begin to diffuse through your skin. If you stay longer, you may find yourself taking photographs of derelict buildings or disused machinery. Or you may start to feel an urge to write a letter to a former lover who left you several years ago, suddenly and without explanation, to tell him about an old harvester you found rusting in the corner of a field. You may feel compelled to write to him because who else would understand how beautiful it is, with the bird's nest where the driver's seat once was and the wheels netted in with weeds?

If this occurs, it means that Pennsylvania has seeped inside you surreptitiously, and it is time to leave.

The official motto of the state of Pennsylvania is: "When in doubt, breathe, but not through your mouth."

VERMONT

Once a year the people of Vermont all go out of their houses and shout "Chimney Witch, Be Gone!" at the top of their lungs. This occurs in early November and is the best time of the year to visit. The tradition originated in the French Acadian culture, which filtered down from the territory that is now Quebec into the state's remote but beautiful Northeast Kingdom. According to legend, the Chimney Witch squats in the chimneys of unsuspecting householders and prevents St. Nicholas from entering the dwelling unless she is given notice to get out before the first frost. This is the only time that Vermonters shout in public and all of them do it simultaneously at 4:00 p.m. on the first Wednesday of the month. A witty local writer commented, apropos of this practice, that in left-wing Vermont even the evil spirits are given almost two months' notice before they are evicted from their abodes.

For people from our country this tradition may seem very strange, since as a rule we dislike loud voices and raucous noise, and our public ceremonies tend to be dignified and quiet. But many visitors say they find the Vermonters' shouting strangely comforting, especially the way that the sound echoes off the faces of the mountains, which makes it sound like the hills are calling back.

In America, Vermont is considered unusually liberal, and this outlook is a point of pride for the state. Although there have been some difficulties between longtime residents, who hold more traditional views, and newcomers, most communities have been able to find common ground. The MJ Dairy incident is a case in point. MJD produces the infamous Mary Jane line of cheeses, all of which contain the resin of the cannabis plant among their ingredients and are said to have a mild narcotic effect. When the dairy's buildings were burned down last year by arsonists, it united libertarians and liberals who believe in marijuana legalization with law-and-order conservatives who don't like to see Vermont become the ground for lawless violence. Prayer vigils were held outside the torched buildings, and within a month enough money had been collected to rebuild the facility from public donations alone.

Vermont has been reforested in the last century, and its trees are still skinny and young. They cling to the granite sides of its mountains as best they can, but life is hard in this cold northern clime. Their roots snoop around the tumble of gray rocks and the thin soil, looking for a way in. Sometimes they find one, but not very often, and when they do manage to puncture the hard shell that the land here habitually wears, they sometimes don't like what they find underneath.

The trees whisper messages among themselves, but they are not old enough yet to have anything more profound to say than human beings do, so it is not advisable to spend much time listening to them. The mountains by contrast are exceedingly old. But they don't talk very often.

NORTH DAKOTA

North Dakota is not a place that most tourists would think to stop, but we recommend it for several reasons of which we give details below.

When you leave Vermont, drive west. Go around those enormous lakes through Ohio, Indiana, Wisconsin and Minnesota. Eventually, you will come to a place that is as flat and empty as an ocean. Stop at a restaurant by the side of the road and order something to eat. Ask the couple sitting in the booth next to you where you are. If they look first at each other and then back at you and then the man of the couple sighs deeply, like his heart might break from disappointment, you will be sure you are in North Dakota.

People in this state are known for their absent-mindedness. They have a tendency to think of things they ought to have said or done after it is much too late to change them: *Oh well,* they are often heard to say. *Next time.* The official state gesture involves clapping the heel of the right hand to the forehead once, as though you are just remembering some task you were supposed to already have finished. The state police do this in unison at their swearing-in ceremonies and accompany it with an extended exhalation of breath in the form of a long "o" (as in "zoo" or "fool"). It is a sight to behold.

No one in North Dakota is completely sure where the land underneath them came from, since it seems to be younger than the rest of the continental United States. There are two competing theories among scientists who study the subject. One holds that the land was an ancient asteroid shaped like a plate. Another proposes that the land in fact remained deep underground for many millennia before a seismic shift thrust it up in a single cataclysmic movement toward the light. The evidence is inconclusive. The fossil record shows animals from vastly different eras crammed together into a single stratum of rock, and this remains unexplained by either theory. Perhaps in North Dakota old forms of life find a final harbor before dying off at last to make room for what is new.

The most beautiful thing in North Dakota is the blue lightning, which, because of the flatness of the terrain, can be seen from hundreds of miles in any direction. It sutures together the clouds and the ground, and in this way it reminds people of the compromises they make between the part of them that wants to stay but flies away, and the part of them that wants to fly away but crouches on the ground, blinking its eyes and licking the air.

After you have seen enough of this marvelous spectacle, continue heading west until you reach Montana.

MONTANA

From space, Montana looks like a supine lion covered in its golden fur. In fact, if you put your hand on the earth in certain places in this state, the ground does omit warmth like the side of a cat flopped down in a square of sunlight. If you see the earth shuddering very gently in and out or hear the deep thrumming noise that might be the hills purring, this is only an illusion—though it is an extremely convincing one.

Montana is known for its vast rangelands that have supported herds of cattle since the state was first settled by Europeans, and its culture centers on cows. People pursue a number of pastimes involving these versatile animals, including cow-racing, cow-vaulting, and the cow-toss. A recent attempt to bring these sports to a wider audience through television has not diminished the specifically local flavor of the contests, and many Montana natives consider these pursuits integral to their way of life.

Montana is one of the few female states in the Union. While there are many states that take the "-a" ending, usually considered feminine, only Georgia and Montana and Maine are actually female. Many people find this information surprising. They are shocked to discover both the scarcity of female states and the fact that Montana—with its pioneer culture valorizing physical strength and emotional reserve—should in fact be one of this small number. This reflects more on our contemporary expectations of male and female than on the state of Montana, which, after all, cannot help how it was made.

HITCHHIKERS

As you continue westward, you will see many people hitchhiking along the roadside and you may wish to pick them up. Usually you can do this without problems: they are mostly young people for whom this is an inexpensive way to see the country. However, there are a few things to be careful of when picking up hitchhikers. Some of them may smell. Some of them may have bad taste in music. Some of them may tell untruths. Several accounts have come back to us about a hitchhiker who is often seen just outside of Billings, a man in a long, midnight-blue coat. According to the rumors, if you pick him up, this man will seem perfectly friendly and benign at first. But eventually he will try to convince you that you must, absolutely, without fail, go and see the state of Louisiana right away. He is persuasive on this subject, extolling the beauties and interests of the place, its history, its unique culture, in an almost mesmerizing tone that makes you feel you cannot miss it, that you must go there immediately.

More than a few travelers have followed his advice. But we must warn you: Do not become one of them. Do not listen to this man. It will lead only to frustration, unnecessary expense and wasted time.

The reason for this is explained below.

LOUISIANA

There is no state of Louisiana. The fact that the myth of its existence persists so powerfully to this day can be attributed to the deep-seated desire we all share for a place between the water and the land that is simultaneously both and neither. In this place we are free to drift over a surface still and dark like glass, which parts before the painted prow of our small wooden boat. It is important that the boat is wooden so we can hear the creaking sound it makes as it eases through channels the color of licorice and among tangled vines trailing luminous moss. Our destination is a small lonely building, a house or sometimes an old general store or even a cantina hoisted above the water by broad stilts under each corner. What we find there differs from person to person. Sometimes the house is empty. Sometimes it is filled with people having a party and dancing. Sometimes there is only a single person waiting on the dock that extends out in front of the building, sitting as though they would have remained exactly in that spot for however long it took us to find them.

The other reason that the state of Louisiana continues to loom so large in our collective imagination is the Great Hoax of 1782. The hoax was orchestrated by a group of planters from the French West Indies who intended to entice capital investment in their enterprises from bankers in Paris and other European cities. They began to spread information about great and growing port cities along the southern coast of the North American mainland, which, they claimed, would soon precipitously increase the trade between the United States, then a recently formed nation, and the islands of the Caribbean. They named these cities after cities in France and even went so far as to have woodcuts and etchings made illustrating the various street scenes and public works then supposedly taking place in them. The artists they hired were talented and they evoked from nothing but their imaginations bustling, vibrant towns inhabited by people from all the nations of the world, mixing and living freely together—a spectacle that at the time had never been witnessed before. Soon it became *au courant* in the French capital to pepper one's speech with slang purported to originate in the Gulf cities. Where this slang truly comes from no one knows, though it shows similarities to the Basque language and also to Welsh.

The campaign was a success. The investors in Europe were moved to open their purses, and money flowed to the French island colonies. But another unforeseen effect also resulted from the machinations of the conspirators, which was the increased interest on the part of the United States in acquiring this rich territory adjacent to its own. As we all know, the Louisiana Purchase of 1803 took place a mere twenty years after the planters first gathered together over port and cigars to devise their plan. Once this purchase was made, of course, the Americans soon discovered their error: there were no Gulf cities. Louisiana was a pure fabrication. But so many among the new revolutionary elite had staked their reputations on the purchase of this territory, including of course Thomas Jefferson himself, that they could hardly admit this publicly. To protect the president's dignity, the fiction was maintained. As it is to this very day.

If, despite our warnings, you travel to the place where Louisiana is supposed to be, you will find nothing but a few placards and signs and a Quonset hut containing an exhibition about the myth. This will doubtless be disappointing and upsetting. One way that Americans sometimes express their negative emotions is by assaulting inanimate objects; for this reason, you might want to kick one of the signs and shout an expletive at the top of your lungs to make yourself feel better. Don't worry if a group of tourists nearby look over at you disapprovingly; glaring silently is also part of the culture.

After that, do not spend any more time in this place. It will only make your already-bad feelings worse. Instead, we advise you to get back in your car and drive away as quickly as you can within the posted speed limits.

NEVADA

If a garbage can was flat, it would be called Nevada. This is what people in surrounding states say when they wish to disparage the state known variously as the Radiation State, the Dust State, and the Slot Machine State (this last is used only by non-Nevadans seeking to provoke Nevadans to fight them in a bar).

While these names are clearly intended to be pejorative, it must be acknowledged that Nevada is the place to which many of America's worst nightmares are eventually consigned. It might be more accurately called the Nation's Unconscious: it is where the American people put the things that they don't want messing up their lawns. The most important of these are nuclear waste and the sex trade.

An odd confluence between these two domains has been remarked upon recently by a well-known pornographer. In both erotic arousal and radiation poisoning the subject undergoes an experience of melting, as internal boundaries and membranes give way allowing for the delirious loosening and mixing of the body's tissues and fluids at an ever-accelerating rate. The dermis separates into its many tenuous layers and peels away, shed like a lizard's scales. The soft tissue becomes tender and swollen as bruises. The limbs lose their rigidity and swim through the suddenly soft air, their motions freed of all consequence, closed off by darkness from any constraint or from the onerous weight of the future until finally the subject itself disperses in death or in "the little death."

Our pornographer further submits that because Nevada is a desert, a place in which time does not appear to pass, we have reserved it as the place in which we collapse gently in on ourselves.

Most of the state is uninhabitable because it lacks water. Visitors slide through it in silver cars on the single great highway to traverse its northern expanse, and they get out to gaze with rapt horror at the emptiness, thinking: *If you wanted to die, all you would have to do is choose a direction and walk.* Numerous attempts to establish towns along this highway have failed, and their remains can be seen at the side of the road, where off-ramps lead to nothing but shuttered and derelict buildings, mostly convenience stores and gas stations. These buildings take several years to be covered by dust completely, and it is possible to judge the building's age by how far up the front door the sand has crept. On our most recent journey through Nevada we saw many buildings in this state of half-submersion, but we did not stop long enough to check their age. There is a slight risk when you do this that you will want to lie down inside one of them until you are covered up by drifts of pale gold earth. If you do this you will not reach the last and most amazing stop on your journey: California.

CALIFORNIA

The beauty of California is famous throughout the world. The sun shines almost every day. There are yellow and brown beaches where the glass-blue ocean shatters on the shore over and over and the sea-birds riot in the air above. The mountains are a gray spine shouldering through the center of the state, offering magnificent views. There is the dry, medicinal smell of eucalyptus and along the northern coast there are the great trees, large as cetaceans, with wood the color of bricks or blood and sharp needles all over to ward off predators. Scientists have recently discovered that these trees seem to be sending a gentle but persistent signal upward into the sky on a frequency that human beings can hardly detect even with our most advanced instruments, but what the signal says they cannot yet decipher.

In spite of all this beauty, there is another, darker side to California that lurks beneath the pleasant surface and occasionally pushes its way up into the light. If you go to the border in the south you will see an example of what we are referring to. For many years, there was a fence that ran along the border to keep people from coming into the country to look for work without the proper papers or permission. A few years ago, this fence was taken down and an invisible, electric barrier erected in its place. If a person tries to cross the border, in spite of the many warnings posted in a multitude of languages, he now receives a huge electric shock, strong enough to send him sailing backward through the air onto his own side of the line. For a while after El Oscuro (as the barrier is known on the Mexican side) first went up, there were protests. People suffered damage to their nerves because of the strong current; some young children who could not read the warning signs were hurt. But instead of taking down the barrier, the government put up a loudspeaker system so that those too young or not fortunate enough to be able to read could be warned to keep away. Since then there have been fewer injuries and the protests have died down as people have become distracted by other things supposedly more pressing.

We advise you to stay away from the border. Although it is not dangerous for you (you are not that kind of foreigner) the experience is upsetting and may ruin your impression of this otherwise bewitching place.

After you have spent some time in California, you may feel you would like to stay forever. This is common among travelers from our country, where the weather is gloomy and cold and where, in the winter, it gets dark early in the afternoon. We arrive in California and are whirled around by the ubiquity of light, the trees that the sea wind has twisted into dark green candle flames, the way the ocean stretches out ahead of you as if it might go on forever. We feel elated, weightless and amazed. We feel that everyone we meet is someone we loved when we were very young and have not seen for years.

This condition has come to be referred to as Golden Fever, and once it sets in it is difficult to shake. Our own researchers have sometimes fallen victim to it, and several of them have never returned home. To combat Golden Fever, there are now quite a few companies that make a business out of kidnapping foreign visitors whose families have become concerned about them. If your family hires one of these, masked men will come for you in the middle of the night and put a sack over your head, then drive you to the airport and put you on a plane that's flying east. Unfortunately, this sudden departure can lead to withdrawal symptoms in certain travelers. In the back of the book, we provide a list of hospitals that can help you recover if you find yourself deprived of California and unable to cope emotionally with the shock.

After several months of treatment, most of the afflicted are able to recover some sense of proportion and resume their ordinary lives. They will remember the feelings of mysterious elation they experienced as if they heard about them secondhand. Their memories of California will seem like photographs, static and arrested and somehow no longer their own. Eventually, they will be just the way they were before, as if they had never been away at all, except occasionally, when they will stare out the window at the heavy sky and early dark and start to cry.

Even travelers from our country who are happy to be home may experience some strange emotions after they return. They may look around at our narrow streets and houses, our landscape that has been green and domesticated for a thousand years, or they may listen to the matter-of-fact way our people talk, their modest aspirations, their tendency to mock all that is too grand, and feel that there is something missing. This feeling will wear off after a while. For America, with all its beauty and variety, is wonderful to visit but not a place you'd really want to live. It lacks the substance and continuity of older, more established nations. Sometimes it seems to tremble like it might vanish at any moment; other times it seems like it is an imitation of a country, a set that will be taken down by a team of stagehands after you pass through it. After you have left, you may wonder whether it was real at all or just a trick of light and water, a mirage, a dream that you aren't sure how to interpret. Was it good or bad or something else entirely? Most people who have been there find it is impossible to say for sure.

Three Marriages

1.

Shortly after they moved from their own house in Darien, Connecticut, into a retirement home near Fort Myers, Florida, Lucinda announced that she didn't want to be married anymore to Fred, her husband of fifty-nine years. When she told her children this, they were first horrified and then dismissive. She could not mean it, they said to her and to each other. She could not possibly be serious. They interpreted it as a sign that she was becoming senile, that her mind and judgment, which had until then remained very sharp, were becoming impaired. They took her to get tested for other signs of reduced cognitive functioning, but the doctors they spoke with found Lucinda to be lucid and competent, her memory of recent and distant events remarkably intact for someone of her age, which was eighty-three years old.

"But what about this idea that she's going to leave my father?" her son Harry asked the gerontologist who administered the battery of tests. "If that doesn't count as crazy, I don't know what does."

The doctor looked at him and shrugged.

"I can't comment on whether your mother is making a sensible choice in this matter," he said. "But she is able to talk about her decision with perfect clarity. Being sane is in no way related to being wise."

"But what do you think we should do about it?" her elder daughter Karen asked.

"There isn't anything you can do," the doctor said. "I suggest you take her home."

So they did and for a while they didn't hear anything further about Lucinda's plans to leave her husband. They decided among themselves that her desire must have been a passing fancy, a phase, a strange fit that she has gone through as a result of her recent move.

But it was not. About a month later, with the reluctant help of her younger daughter Cynthia, Lucinda moved her belongings out of the apartment she and Fred shared in the Golden Years Retirement Community and got her own apartment in another, similar community nearby. She petitioned for a legal separation. She spoke to a lawyer about filing for divorce.

Her children were furious with her. One after another they came to see her, her two daughters and one son, and they told her how angry her decision had made them, how selfish they thought she was being. How could she leave her husband now? Their father, they said, was old and not very well. He'd been through treatment for cancer a couple of years before, which no one thought he would survive. But he had survived it and recovered, although he never gained back all the strength he lost during his chemotherapy. Every day during that difficult time, Lucinda had gone with him to the hospital where he would be wheeled down the corridor by the same strong and friendly nurse with long blonde hair and peppermint-pink lipstick to the treatment room. Then Lucinda would wait while he was given the dose of chemicals and afterwards she would accompany him home. And in all that time she never faltered, never expressed impatience with him, was as steady and devoted as it is possible to be. When the doctor reported his tumor gone, she celebrated with the whole family, and since then none of her friends or relatives had detected anything significantly wrong or altered between her and her husband. Why, then, was she leaving him now?

Lucinda did not answer them, at least not in the way they wished to be answered. She merely said that it was what she wanted and she was sorry if it hurt them but she had to do what made her happy with what she had left of her own life. Then she smiled and changed the subject to something trivial and pleasant: the flowers she was planting in her window boxes, the outings she took with her friends to go shopping and to the movies. She seemed content.

For his part, Fred was extremely upset and bewildered by Lucinda's decision to leave; he could offer his children no insight at all into what had happened between him and their mother. After Lucinda moved out, he remained living in the apartment they had shared, surrounded by the belongings they had acquired through their long years together: the many souvenirs from their trips abroad, the photographs of their children, the gifts they'd been given by friends—a hundred daily reminders of his wife's vanished presence. After his initial shock, he settled into a solitary routine; he would breakfast alone, then spend the morning reading the paper. Then he would go down and swim slowly up and down the pool in the recreation center until he was tired. Then he would have dinner with other people from the retirement community, friends, or sometimes one of his kids. He rarely had to dine alone. Occasionally he would run into his wife in one of the restaurants in the complex or in the community center where classes and lectures and musical events were held. The first few times this happened, she approached and asked him how he was. But since he either glared silently at her or stood up and walked away without a word, she soon stopped trying to be friendly and ignored him, too. This went on for several months. But one day, when he came back from supper, he found a note that had been slid under the door of his apartment. It said: *Come and meet me by the lake.* It was in Lucinda's handwriting. He read it over, surprised, and decided to follow its directions. There was an ornamental lake on the grounds of the retirement complex and he put on his coat and went down in the elevator and walked over to it. He saw Lucinda waiting on a bench looking out over the smooth surface of the water. She was half-lit by the lamps that stood on posts alongside the footpath, and something about the way she was sitting made him remember how she had looked when they first met: tall and slender with an upright, formal posture and tidy movements and gestures. He came and sat beside her on the bench. Then he could see that her face was not the face of the young woman he remembered; it was lined, the skin delicate and fissured with veins. She turned to look at him.

She said: "I found the letters."

For a moment he couldn't think of what she meant.

"What letters?" he asked. She didn't reply. Then it came to him.

When he'd been a young man, shortly after he was married, he had developed an infatuation for a woman at the insurance office where he worked. There had been letters exchanged, a brief affair conducted in hotel rooms around town, then contrition and a return to his marriage from which he had never strayed again. Shortly after the affair, his former mistress had moved to another state. Lucinda had never even suspected anything as far as he could tell, and he had not felt compelled to confess to her because the affair had never meant very much to him and was not a sign of any deep unhappiness at home so much as an accident of circumstance and immaturity—in other words, a mistake.

But for some reason he had kept the letters. He did not know why, but he had kept them locked in the top drawer of the desk in his study through all his and Lucinda's subsequent years together. And sometimes when they were fighting or when they were at odds with each other, he would go into his office and touch the handle of the drawer where the letters were and this would make him feel stronger, separate from his wife, a person with a secret. He felt the need to do this less and less as they aged, until he almost forgot about the letters altogether. Sometimes he would think of them and say to himself that he really should get rid of them, but he never got around to actually throwing them away; it just never seemed that important. In fact, the letters and the affair they chronicled seemed so insignificant that, when they moved the last time and he sold the desk, he had not felt it necessary to take any special steps to hide them. At their age, what did it matter? It was so long ago that he could not remember the woman's face, only that she'd had dyed red hair and a birthmark down near her collarbone; sometimes he could not even recall her name right away. So he put the letters in a box along with other books and papers; he had not thought of them again until this minute.

"Is that what this is all about?" he asked. "That's ridiculous."

Lucinda shrugged. "I knew that would be what you'd say. I knew the children would say that too. That's why I didn't tell you until everything was arranged for us to separate."

Fred persisted: "But don't you see? It doesn't matter now—it didn't even matter at the time. Why didn't you tell me that was the problem? Are you really that angry at me for something that happened so long ago?" He paused from speaking and an idea came to him: "Are you angry with me because I didn't tell you? Because I kept the secret all this time?" he asked.

"No," Lucinda said. "That isn't it, either. I was unhappy to find that you'd had a love affair, of course. And I was also upset that you kept it secret for so long. But those things I could have forgiven, I think.

"It was when I saw that you had stopped trying to hide the letters from me that I knew you no longer thought that I was a person capable of jealousy. You had stopped thinking about me as a woman and had begun to see me as just an old person who shouldn't feel the same things as other people. If that is true then what is the point of being married?"

"For companionship," Fred said. "To keep us from being alone. Because it's better than nothing."

Lucinda looked at him but didn't answer. Then she stood up and smoothed down her skirt with both her hands. Without speaking another word, she turned away and walked along the lakeside path back toward the apartment building where she now lived and she did not turn around to look at him again.

2.

Karen and David were considered by their friends and families to be as close to a perfect couple as any of them had ever known. Both attractive but not so beautiful that it overwhelmed their other qualities, both clever but not unbalanced by a particular extraordinary talent or passionate calling, they met in college in New England, where they were students at a prestigious private school with a reputation for its programs in foreign languages and literature and for its proximity to wonderful ski resorts which the students often visited when they weren't busy studying. They met in a class on Russian literature in translation. They dated during their final year as undergraduates and found that they had many things in common. They both liked hiking and tennis; they both had studied French and liked to travel. After they graduated they went together to do a year of social-service work in a school in rural Senegal, then moved to New York, where David began law school and Karen got a job in the editorial department of a women's magazine. With help from their parents they bought an apartment in Manhattan. They married the fall that David took the bar and got his first job working for a big law firm headquartered in midtown.

They lived like this for several years, David working at the law firm and Karen editing articles about interior design and fashion and women who ran nonprofit organizations in countries in the developing world. They had lots of friends in the city who had gone to the same college as them and whom they often met for drinks or dinner and with whom they went away for long weekends at the beach or up to Vermont to ski. They visited with Karen's parents Lucinda and Fred at their house up in Connecticut often; David's parents, who lived out in Colorado, did not like New York and did not come to visit much. David worked longer hours than he would have liked, and Karen felt from time to time that her job did not provide enough of an intellectual challenge for her. But generally they considered themselves to be very happy. They talked in a noncommittal way about starting a family in a few years' time.

One day, Karen was at home in their apartment by herself. She was looking for a page she'd forgotten to bookmark on the browser of the computer in the second bedroom, which they used as a home office/exercise room when they didn't have guests staying with them. The page she was looking for had the pattern for a sweater she was going to knit for David for his birthday and she couldn't remember the name of the site where she had seen it. She was scrolling through the history file when she noticed an address that made her stop her search. The name in the URL was so strange and unexpected—www.pleasehitme.com—that she clicked on it before she thought about what she was doing. The screen winked and shifted and the site began to load, background first, then rows of images popping into view one after another.

What she saw upset her right away. The page was filled with pictures of men and women, naked or nearly so, displaying various kinds of injuries on their faces and their bodies: black eyes, split and swollen lips, torn skin. Some of their injuries had obviously been inflicted by other human beings—bruises the size and shape of fingers, parallel gouges left by fingernails—while others were just maps of unexplained damage. Some of the men and women wore handcuffs or were tied with rope. But the pictures she found herself looking at most intently showed just expanses of blued and purpled flesh, lacerations and incisions in the smooth sheet of the skin, in which the faces of the subjects were not even visible, only the pale or dark angles of their bodies with their hair and creases, the shapes of the flesh and the bone beneath and the saturated colors of the wounds.

Karen stared in disbelief. She was not naive about the existence of pornography online and she would not have been especially shocked to find a link to a site showing posed and naked women that her husband had been looking at. She would not have been pleased exactly but she would not have been surprised; in fact, she would not have cared about it very much at all. She might have closed the window feeling mild annoyance or disappointment; she might have forgotten it by the time David came home later that evening.

But this was different. This she would not be able to forget, not only because the images were appalling in and of themselves but because there was nothing that she knew about the man she lived with that could help her understand what she was seeing. In all the years she'd known him, David had never shown any propensity for physical violence toward himself or others; the most forceful thing he'd ever done in her presence was to slam a heavy book down on a table once when they were arguing; he'd certainly never raised his hand to her. He did not like grisly films, did not play video games involving gruesome violence or slaughter. He even found piercings and tattoos distasteful because of the association that they had with pain.

Karen sat at the computer with the mutilated bodies and ecstatic-looking faces illuminated in front of her and for several minutes she had no idea what to do. She could not unsee what she had seen. She stood up and walked around the apartment in a circle then decided to go out for a walk to try to clear her head. She shut off the computer and picked up her purse and took the elevator down to the street and walked in a daze in the direction of the park. She was so distracted that she didn't look carefully where she was going and, crossing Amsterdam Avenue, she stepped off the curb and into the path of a taxi that was racing through a yellow light. The driver swerved trying to avoid her, but he did not change course fast enough and the left side of his fender collided with her legs.

She felt the initial impact of the car as something personal, malicious, a giant force that seemed to come out of the air and shove her whole body angrily up and forward. Then she felt the pain of impact as she hit the ground. Her consciousness seemed to splinter and after that she remembered only fragments of what happened, flashbulb instants: the paramedics cutting off her clothes, people shouting, the stretcher she was lying on being loaded into the ambulance, the siren starting up as they began to move. Later she learned that she had broken her jaw and one side of her collarbone when she hit the ground. In the ambulance she lost consciousness altogether.

When she woke up, David was there. He was sitting beside her bed, holding her hand. He saw she was awake and stood up so that she didn't have to move her head to look into his face. He was staring at her with an expression of anxiety and tenderness more intense than any she had seen before, and for a moment she was flooded with simple relief at seeing him and gratitude that he was there. Then she remembered the events that had led up to her accident, and the bruised and bloodied faces from the screen came into her mind as vividly as though she had seen them only a moment before.

She looked up at her husband, his gentle, rapt expression and her stomach turned. Was he looking at her or at the damage she had suffered? She could picture how she looked right now: her face swollen up and lacerated where she had fallen on the pavement. She closed her eyes and tried to swallow but the muscles in her throat ached when she tried to move them and her mouth was as dry as paper. Her head was throbbing and her jaw ached and her whole body felt like one gigantic bruise. She closed her eyes wanting the world to go away.

"Sweetheart," David was saying somewhere above her. "I'm so sorry." But she knew he did not mean that he was sorry for anything he had done, only that he regretted what had happened. Then he bent to kiss her on the forehead. She saw his face lowering toward her, his eyes sorrowful and his lips pressed together and she tried to tell him not to touch her but found it hurt too much to speak. She made a noise in the back of her throat that sounded to her like the shapeless noise a drowning person might make.

"The doctors said you shouldn't try to speak until your jaw has had time to heal some," David said as he looked at her and bent again to kiss her. She shrank away from him to the far side of the narrow bed but she couldn't move far enough away to avoid him. When he kissed her she felt his lips linger on her skin. She found that her left arm moved pretty well and she raised it even though it hurt and pushed him away. He looked bewildered and she knew he didn't understand. When he tried to kiss her again, she managed to roll over so that she was facing away from him toward the wall.

"What?" she heard him say. "What's wrong?" But of course she couldn't tell him.

Through the weeks of her recovery, whenever he would try to touch her she would pull away. Even when she was well enough to speak and walk around, as her bruises began to heal and turned from red to purple to black to green and yellow, as her cuts began to heal, she still found that each time he came near her she would think of the pictures she had seen and wonder: does he find me more beautiful now than he did when I was well? She would shy away from him, upset and revolted by this possibility. David for his part responded to her coldness with solicitude and careful, gentle attentiveness, which might have been caused by simple pity for her condition but which seemed to Karen to show that in fact he actually cherished her more in her damaged state than he had before and made her avoid his touch more assiduously than ever. Each gesture he made to demonstrate his affection had the effect of putting more distance between them, more strangeness and silence until she could hardly stand his presence anywhere near her; she would flinch when he touched her, she could not look into his face without crying. She felt too upset and ashamed to tell him what she'd seen on the day before her accident. Too much time had passed, she thought, and she'd caused him too much anxiety by her behavior to tell him now what had occurred; it seemed both too small and too vast to have been the seed of their estrangement.

Even a patient husband could endure only so much of this treatment. By the time Karen's face and body were entirely healed they were barely speaking to each other. While she was recovering, he'd moved into the spare room so she'd be more comfortable at night and he remained there, moving more and more of his belongings out of their old room. He worked longer hours and so they didn't have to dine together. Soon this became normal for them, an established routine. They inhabited the same house but moved around each other like flotsam caught in opposing currents. At a certain point it seemed that at any moment one of them would say out loud what they both knew and then they would separate.

But then, sometimes, Karen would come across David unexpectedly in a room where she had not known he would be. She would remember what it had been like between them before. She wondered if that feeling could ever come back and she would imagine it returning as if it had always existed and had only been away on a long journey. Or David would arrive home at night to find Karen fallen asleep with her book still open on her chest and the bedside lamp still on and, coming in to switch it off, he'd notice the dark storm of her hair on the pillow and think how beautiful it was. And so they would each put off for another day saying that they thought that one of them should leave. And another day. And another. And another.

3.

Cynthia met Kris online during her second year of residency after medical school.

She had decided to apply for a residency in surgery, even though this meant a longer training period and even more lengthy hours and greater stress, because she didn't want to settle for one of the specializations that she considered "mommy track" like dermatology or pediatrics; she wanted to attain the highest level of prestige and skill in her field. When she was accepted to surgery she had felt both thrilled and terrified. She moved to Madison, Wisconsin, after she finished her exams and started her internship at the university hospital there in July.

Of course, she had very little time to socialize or date or to pursue any interests outside work—she'd loved cycling during college and she'd taken several long bicycle trips, including one around the coast of Ireland; she'd played the piano well enough that she'd considered going to a conservatory to study composition and performance; she liked to garden and to cook; but all those things went by the wayside now. She had expected this. She had no time for anything that first year except work and it was thrilling and exhausting. Sometimes she envied the interns who were going into general practice and would be done in a year or two, but other times she pitied them: how could you ever want to leave the intensity of the hospital, a place where you knew the things you did and the decisions you made were of the greatest importance, where you were changing and saving lives every day?

But the body has its own cravings quite apart from the intellect, and sometimes she would feel the absence of a lover in her life as clearly as a hunger pang and then she would wonder if she'd made the right decision. It was not the same for women, she understood; even now, the expectations for a wife were different from those for a husband, and although of course many individual men and women did not conform to traditional roles and found a way to love each other anyway, still when a man she was on a date with learned she was going to be a surgeon or when after a few meetings he found he had to see her only when her work allowed, which was not often, she felt him detach, retrench, withdraw. Sometimes she could tell the exact moment when this happened. Something in the man's posture or in his facial expression changed. The duration of time in which he'd look at her would shorten until at last he didn't look at her at all and then she would get the call or, worse, the email or once even, to her horror, a text message, telling her that he didn't think it was working out between them and he liked her but was sorry, etc.

All the other interns in her track were men and she tried dating a couple of them but they were too much like her: ambitious, focused and competitive.

Then her elderly parents split up, to Cynthia and her siblings' great surprise, at the end of her first year of residency. She had thought that they were happy together or, if not happy, at least content, at least comfortable with each other. Their separation really shook her up; what other model of relationship did she have? Her brother Harry was on his second divorce. Her sister Karen occupied a marriage that seemed great at the beginning but then lost all the air inside it; Karen and her husband David seemed more like ghosts haunting each other than like spouses. Was that the point of all this effort, to end up trapped with someone in a set of small rooms, unable to either leave or truly inhabit your own life?

So Cynthia stopped trying. She focused on her work and when she was working she was happy. There was so much to learn, so much to take in; sometimes she thought she could feel the new pathways of understanding being driven through her brain like roads. She was coming to see the body in ways that she could not have imagined before, to understand how well it could recover from damage and disruption, how adroitly it could compensate when it encountered some unexpected obstacle to the fulfillment of its functions and desires. It seemed to her that this capacity to adapt was its particular gift, its magic. Sometimes she thought she could see through the people around her, through their seemingly inert flesh and into the fizzing, busy miracle of blood and bones and cells remaking and renewing themselves.

She finished her shifts exhausted and most nights or mornings she would come home and crawl into bed and drop into sleep like a stone into a pool of water. But sometimes she was still full of the feverish energy, the adrenaline that had sustained her through the many hours on her feet and then she could not sleep.

On these insomniac nights she poured herself a drink and sat down at her computer and clicked through pages of brightly colored ephemera: news stories about the latest film star to be stopped for reckless driving and ordered into rehab, pictures of children in faraway countries rescued after floods and earthquakes, quizzes that told her which Beatle she would be if she ever had been or ever could be a Beatle. And sometimes she chatted with people whom she'd never met and never thought she would.

In the different chat rooms she would visit, she introduced herself to whoever was already there and described herself a little. She told who she was and what she did, though never exactly where she lived. She talked for a while with the mostly male interlocutors who came her way, and they were variously dull or interesting, intelligent or stupid, charming or crass; she liked each of these qualities or not depending on her mood. Some evenings she was pleased to find herself communicating with someone erudite and cultured about the works of art they both loved and the books they'd read. Other times she was glad when the person typed some blunt obscenity about her breasts or cunt. She replied in kind or closed the window on her screen immediately depending on whether the explicitness turned her on or bored her. Eventually, she started to get sleepy and could go to bed and rest.

This was how she first encountered Kris. The name came up in a chat room for classical music enthusiasts that Cynthia had been to on previous occasions, but she had never seen this user before. *Hello,* she typed. After a moment, the mild reply came: *Hello.*

Who are you? she typed.

My name is Kris, said the screen after a pause. *I live in Norway in a little town north of the capital. Who are you?*

I'm Cynthia. I'm training to be a doctor. I grew up in Chicago.

There was another delay and then: *Chicago? I have been to Chicago several times to perform. I used to play the violin in the symphony in Oslo and we went on a number of tours in the United States.*

What do you do now? Cynthia asked.

A few years ago, I left musical performance so that I could develop and run an organic farm. I thought: how hard can that be after learning to play Shostakovich? Serves me right! Farming is so much harder than I could ever have imagined when I started out. It took all my time! Finally, though, it is beginning to turn a profit and I have hired a manager to help me run it so that I can go back to the city almost every weekend. Which is good because I can see my kids more often.

You have children?

Two. A boy and a girl. They live with my ex.

That must be difficult . . .

Well, we are relatively lucky. She's a wonderful parent and we get on well as friends, we just weren't so good at living together in the end. We were too different. Perhaps you know how that can be . . . There was a blank on the screen, the cursor pulsing as it waited. Then Kris typed: *But I'm sorry, I've talked a lot about myself. Please, tell me about you and your work. Being a doctor must be fascinating . . .*

They continued chatting and when Cynthia finally glanced at the clock she had to excuse herself and go to bed because several hours had passed in what felt like much less time. She had been enjoying their conversation so much that she had not noticed. This pleasure was not only because they had so many interests in common, although that seemed to her remarkable enough: Cynthia felt like she was talking to someone who had taken up all the discarded threads of her own life—music, gardening, Kris even liked cycling—and made another life out of them. But there was also an ease between them, a shared sense of humor. When Kris made jokes, which were mostly gently self-mocking, she found herself laughing in spite of her exhaustion. She liked the slight formality of the way Kris wrote, the sign of someone who had learned English as a second language and knew its grammar too well to be a native speaker. Kris seemed to like her too, and before they signed off at last asked if they could meet again the following evening. Cynthia checked her schedule and agreed and they set a time and said goodnight.

Away from the screen, she felt light and graceful as she got ready for bed that night as though someone she could not see was observing her benignly and approvingly.

The next night they met again and the conversation was just as interesting. She wrote about her decision not to pursue music and her work at the hospital. She told Kris things that she had told to no one else: how upset she'd been by her parents' late divorce, how she felt she had to work twice as hard as other people to compensate for being shy and serious and awkward. Again the time flew by. For the next week they chatted every night, even when Cynthia got home very late, and their rapport grew flirtatious. They swapped photographs (she spent some time and effort choosing which one to send) and she was pleased with what she saw: a picture of a blond man with high cheekbones and a prominent nose and slightly craggy brows that she thought looked dignified and that kept his face from being too pretty, which she would not have liked. His skin was creased around the eyes and mouth; he looked in the picture both capable of laughter and capable of great seriousness and concentration. She printed out a small copy of the picture and put it in her wallet in the space with the clear plastic window where other people put pictures of their spouses or their kids. She would take it out and look at it whenever she wanted to feel a little burst of energy and pleasure.

All week she flew around as though the force of gravity had been temporarily diminished and she was lighter than she'd been the week before. Her work went particularly well and she was praised by the attending physician, who commended her in front of the other residents. She felt the two things must be connected: her late-night chats with Kris and her good performance at work. She thought she must work up the courage to ask whether a visit would be possible: she could go to Norway or Kris could come to Wisconsin. That night, on screen, she read: *I would like to invite you to come and visit me here. Whenever it is convenient for you, I would love to meet you in person. You can come for as long as you like.*

She typed back: *You read my mind. I was just about to invite you to come and visit me.*

They settled that Cynthia would come to Norway, since she had a short vacation coming up. Kris would come down to Oslo and meet her at the airport. They could spend a couple of days there and then go up to the farm if they wanted to. Kris bought the ticket that night and sent the itinerary to Cynthia. When she opened the message, she felt her heart leap, her pulse quicken. That night she had her first dream about Kris. It was not overtly sexual. They were sitting together on a mountainside, green and bare of trees. Kris reached out and laid both hands on her knee, and this was what she remembered when she woke: how beautiful those hands were, how distinct, with long fingers, strong and elegant, but not unscathed. She woke up with them still before her eyes, imagining what it would be like to be touched by them.

One evening of the following week, Cynthia was having dinner in a Chinese restaurant across the street from the hospital with a couple of the other residents after their shift. When it came time to pay, she opened her wallet to take out her debit card and left it lying unfolded on the table beside her while she looked over the check. The woman sitting beside her, whose name was Sonya, glanced over and said:

"Why do you have a picture of Amund Eilertsen in your wallet?"

"What?" Cynthia said, confused.

"Amund Eilertsen, the actor. That's a picture of him." And she pointed to the photograph behind the plastic window.

Cynthia felt her stomach plummet through the floor. She felt like she could hardly breathe. "Oh," she managed to say. "It's a joke. My sister gave it to me. I used to like him when I was younger and she'd tease me about it and so, you know . . ." She trailed off and smiled in a way she hoped covered the turmoil inside her.

Sonya said: "He was always on TV when we would go to Sweden to visit my grandparents, but hardly anyone in this country has even seen anything he's been in, since he hasn't done many films. What did you see him in?"

"I can't even remember. It was so long ago . . ." The waiter was handing out the receipts and she took hers and absorbed herself in signing it, figuring the tip. She didn't look at Sonya because she thought that if she did, she might start to cry. When the checks were brought back to the table, she said that she was feeling completely exhausted and excused herself to go. She was halfway down the block to her car when she heard someone call her name behind her. She turned around and saw Sonya coming after her holding Cynthia's purse in her hand: she'd departed in such a hurry she had left it on the back of her chair.

When she arrived home it was nearly midnight, the hour when she usually spoke with Kris—or whoever that was, she thought. She understood suddenly, sickeningly, that the words on the screen could have come from anyone; she had no way to know whether the person with whom she had become so quickly and intensely involved even lived in Norway, had been a musician or a farmer or a parent. The shared interests had seemed genuine; Kris had known more than she about music and cultivating plants. The descriptions of journeys by bicycle they'd shared had been so detailed and the pleasure taken in them so similar that they couldn't possibly be entirely made up . . . could they? Also the things they did not share: Kris's manner of talking about being a parent was one of humor and affection, and the frustrations and triumphs of running a small business had seemed true. Last week on a whim she had looked up the brand of organic produce that was supposed to come from Kris's farm and it was real enough, but of course anyone could have looked up that website, used its details. The fact that the farm was real proved nothing.

A pang of sadness and disappointment burst inside her chest. Their affinity had seemed so genuine. But the face of the person she had thought she was falling in love with belonged to someone else entirely, some actor whom she'd never seen.

Why would someone do that, create a whole persona that

was not their own? What possible motivation could they have for doing such a thing?

She considered simply vanishing, never again logging into the chat room where they used to meet, blocking any messages that arrived from Kris. But she decided that she couldn't simply leave things unresolved. She poured herself an extra-large glass of bourbon, sat down at the computer, logged into the chat room and waited. When the name Kris appeared on screen she left the initial greeting sitting on the screen unanswered, until the words *Hello? Are you there?* appeared beside it.

I know that photograph isn't you, she typed. Then she sat back away from the keyboard and waited. For a minute nothing happened. Then the words flashed up:

I'm sorry. I don't know what I was thinking. Everything else I told you has been perfectly true.

How do I know that? Cynthia typed. *How can I believe anything you say?*

Again there was a pause and then:

I understand you must be very angry. I am truly, truly sorry. I thought that if I sent that picture you would continue to talk to me. I did not realize that it would matter until it was too late. I thought that when you came to visit, you would find out then. I thought, somehow, that would be easier.

Easier for who?

I don't know. Easier to make you understand that the other things I've told you are sincere. I'm sorry.

But why did you send me a fake picture at all? Why not just send a real one?

Would you like me to send you one now?

Yes, Cynthia typed, then hesitated and deleted it. *No,* she wrote instead. *How would I know the one you're sending now is real?*

I see your point, Kris typed after a moment. *Look, I understand I have no right to ask you this, but will you consider please coming to Oslo anyway? I will arrange for a hotel; you do not have to stay with me. I would just like to meet you, once. Then you can go back to the United States and never contact me again if you like. I would understand. Please consider it.*

Cynthia hesitated. Then she typed: *I'll have to think about it.*

Fine, Kris typed, *that is fine. Just let me know. When you are ready to do so.*

I'm going to go now, Cynthia typed. *Goodbye.*

Goodbye, Kris said, and vanished from the screen.

For the next week Cynthia did not contact Kris at all, nor did Kris try to contact her. She felt a growing curiosity about this person whose words she'd found so captivating. She was not so much interested in what Kris had hidden. Obviously, whoever she would meet in Oslo would be different from what she'd imagined—maybe a different gender or a different race, perhaps disabled in some way, perhaps much older or much younger than herself. What interested her more was whether she would feel in his or her presence any of the excitement and intimacy she'd felt so strongly in their writing. Had she experienced some real connection to another person? Or had she just been talking to herself? She wanted to find out.

And yet it seemed completely foolish to travel all that way to meet a stranger who had after all misled her. Should she go or not? Days passed and she still could not make up her mind.

Then a few days before her scheduled trip, her mother called. Since she'd helped Lucinda move into her new apartment, they had seen each other only a few times. Cynthia did not have much time to travel and Lucinda found it difficult at her age to come up to Wisconsin, especially during the long, cold winter months. But Lucinda called her regularly once a week and sometimes, recently, they would talk for a long time as they had not done since Cynthia was a child.

This week, when Lucinda asked how her week had been, Cynthia hesitated. She had planned to say that everything was fine. Instead, she found herself on the verge of tears and then talking all about the person she had met online, the invitation and the photograph. She expected Lucinda, who had been so practical about the end of her own marriage, to say that she must forget about Kris and move on as soon as possible. But after Cynthia has finished speaking, she heard Lucinda take a breath and when she spoke her voice was full of strong emotion.

"I think," she said, "you should go."

"You do?" Cynthia was astonished.

"Yes," Lucinda said. "Kris has not been completely open with you, but keeping a secret can sometimes be a sign of love. I'm not saying that it's right to do, but perhaps it is not the worst thing either. Why not go and find out who this person is?" Lucinda said.

The next day Cynthia wrote to Kris and said she'd come to Oslo after all. She thought: whatever happens, at least I'll know. She thought that if she didn't like what she discovered, she could take the train to Stockholm or Copenhagen and spend the weekend exploring there.

As she packed her suitcase for the trip, she felt excitement and nervousness, even though she told herself that there was no reason for her to be anticipating anything. She slept a little on the flight and then woke up as they were taxiing to the terminal at Gardermoen. She walked slowly with her bag along the corridor to passport control. Kris had promised to meet her on the other side of customs and had described the clothes she should look for at the airport: a blue jacket, black trousers and a gray wool scarf. She cleared immigration and rolled her bag through customs. On the far side, there were people lined up waiting for arriving passengers. She scanned the faces of the crowd, searching for someone at once familiar and totally unknown.

She saw the woman standing over to one side of the concourse. She was leaning on the wall and had one leg crossed over the other. She was peering into the stream of arriving passengers, but she had not yet seen Cynthia, so Cynthia had a moment to observe her unobserved herself. The woman had high cheekbones and a kindly mouth and fair skin a little burned from working outdoors. Her sandy hair was tied in a long braid down her back and she looked nervous. Cynthia stopped and stared at her and then the woman caught sight of her and stood up straight, her face lit up with hope. Cynthia found herself walking toward her, leaving her suitcase where it stood and holding out both hands to her. The woman reached out her hands, too, and Cynthia saw that they were fine, long-fingered hands, a violinist's hands, strong, freckled and marked by other kinds of work. She recognized them. They were the same hands from her dream. She reached out and took them in her own.

She stood in the fluorescent lighting of the airport concourse holding hands with this stranger while people passed them on either side.

"It's you," she said, and then again: "It's you."

A Boy My Sister Dated in High School

A boy my sister dated in high school slapped her across the face during an argument. They were sitting in the front seat of his car, parked by the basketball court behind our house, and she made a sarcastic reply to something he had said and before she knew what was happening, he'd raised his hand and swung it, open palmed, against her cheek.

She didn't tell me about this until years later after we had both left home. When she told me, I felt at once angry and strangely guilty because the boy in question was extraordinarily good looking and I remembered having been impressed in a shallow way that I never spoke about that my sister was dating someone so handsome. I was jealous of a lot of things about my sister in those days: her beauty and her ease with people, how spontaneously funny she could be, how well she was liked. She fit in at our school and in our town, in her own body, in a way that I could not seem to manage, quiet and bookish and peculiar as I was then and remain. Still, there was never a time when I didn't love her very much and when I wouldn't have done whatever I could to support and defend her.

Why didn't you tell me sooner? I asked, when she finally told me.

When the boy she was dating hit my sister, it made a sharp cracking sound, just like it does in the movies. She raised her hand and touched the side of her own face. The expanse of skin where he'd struck her buzzed and tingled, felt weirdly alive. It didn't hurt and even the actual slap itself hadn't really hurt. Instead, she was shocked, surprised because she had not expected this, and then confused about what she should do next.

She looked over at the boy she was dating, who had just hit her. He was leaning way back away from her against the car door as if he was afraid, either of her or of what he had just done. In his eyes was an expression of shock and remorse much more intense than anything she herself seemed to be feeling. He too had been surprised, and he looked like he might be about to cry. At that moment it came into her mind that maybe, in punishment for what he had done, the gods had magically frozen him in his current physical position: curled up like a frightened fetus with his eyes bugged out and his mouth hanging slightly open. Perhaps he would be stuck like that forever. In her mind she envisioned having to explain to the boy's mother how her son came to be paralyzed in this posture: *He hit me,* she would say, *and then, well, now he doesn't seem able to move or speak. I'm sorry.* She thought of him in various scenes over the course of his life to come—in school, at home, in church—still fixed in that attitude, and the absurdity of these images together with the amazement she still felt at what had just occurred made her suddenly snort with laughter.

Her laughter seemed to free the boy from his paralysis.

"Oh, god," he said. "I'm so sorry. I'm so, so sorry. I didn't mean . . ." He reached out toward her as though he wanted to take back what he'd done, but then he withdrew his hand. "I'm sorry," he said again. He hung his head.

"I guess you should take me home," my sister said. Suddenly she felt like crying. He nodded and started the car. When they pulled up in front of my parents' house, he turned off the engine. He looked over at her mournfully. She suddenly thought he was making a huge, self-centered melodrama out of something that wasn't really so important. He wanted to be a terrible, unforgivable villain. She did not want to give him that satisfaction.

"Look," she said. "I'm okay. It doesn't hurt. I'm not, like, scarred for life or anything."

"Really?" he asked.

"Really," she said. She leaned over and kissed him on the cheek. He clasped her hands gratefully. They smiled at each other because that was what they were used to doing. When they smiled, it felt as if a moment before they had been drowning in some cold, unpleasant sea, but now they were back on solid ground, back in the world they knew. A wave of relief swept over them.

"You were being kind of a bitch," he said.

"I was," she conceded. "And you were being a class-one a-hole." She opened the door and got out.

"Can I call you tomorrow?" he called after her.

"Yes," she said and went inside. She could hardly even feel where he had hit her at all anymore.

Because they had made up and because she wasn't hurt, she didn't feel like she needed to mention to anyone what had happened. If she said anything to our mother, she thought, Mom would only overreact. She would call the school, maybe the boy's parents. She would say things about violence against women and the patriarchy, the kind of embarrassing things that my sister had to do her best to ignore so that she would not be a total outcast in the conservative suburb where we lived. If she told our mother and she started making a fuss, it would definitely mean that she and the boy would break up and stop dating. They were both part of a big group of friends, and she didn't want to cause problems in that group over something that was really, truly no big deal but that might become a big deal if the parents were involved. It wasn't like she was some battered and abused woman, like you saw on television talk shows or heard about on local news. Probably, in a few months, she wouldn't even remember that it had happened.

So she said nothing and the boy never did it again and after a while they broke up for unrelated reasons and started dating other people without much drama or distress to either of them. They finished high school, went on to different colleges. They didn't keep in touch.

But during that time, unlike what she had expected, the

memory of being hit by the boy didn't just fade away and vanish. It wasn't that she thought about it all the time or it ruined her life or she could never trust a man again or anything like that. From time to time it would come into her mind, that day, the moment of surprised confusion afterward. And she came to feel, especially as she got a little older, that she had let herself down by the way she had reacted. This was the feeling that grew incrementally inside her. She should not have tried to make him feel better by telling him it was no big deal. She should not have kept it from their friends just so they could all continue to get along. From the beginning she had failed to stand up for herself, and now she knew, or felt like she knew, about herself that she would let someone do that to her and do nothing about it. She would be obliging. She would comply.

This guilt about how she hadn't stood up for herself was like a small stone that she had to carry around. That was how she pictured it. Small and round, but heavy. And she came to believe—she said, when she finally told me about it all those years later—that maybe if she told people about it, as she was doing now, it would get smaller and lighter; that sharing would diminish it, make it smaller, maybe even make it vanish.

And I thought, but did not say: maybe, or maybe it will make it multiply.

My Daughter and Her Spider

After her father moved away, my daughter Lisa had a difficult few months. She slept badly. She had terrible nightmares from which she'd wake up shouting words I couldn't understand or crying tears of fright. She threw tantrums that would come over her like fits and then she'd cry until she was exhausted, hoarse and dizzy. I worried constantly about her. I wasn't in particularly great shape myself after the ending of my marriage. I was working longer hours so that I could pay our bills. I was tired all the time, struggling to keep from slipping down into my own sadness and drowning there.

I wanted to be strong and do the right thing for my daughter. But I really didn't know how to help her cope.

Dr. Clemens, the psychologist I took her to, suggested that we get her a Companion. She gave me the name and address of a facility where we could go to pick one out. She said they'd have a full range of choices, each one carefully engineered to meet the needs of children who had recently been through a traumatic loss.

I was skeptical at first.

"What about a real pet?" I remember asking.

Dr. Clemens sighed. She'd obviously had this question from parents many times before. "Well," she said, "we generally recommend artificial over natural. The children bond with them just as well and there's no mess, no allergies, a lot less noise. The schools prefer it; some will even let the children bring Companions into class with them."

She handed me a brochure. On the cover were pictures of the company's designs: a sleek, elegant, azure-colored cat; a dog with shaggy, silver hair. Their faces looked alert and curious. You could hardly tell that they were just machines.

"All right," I said. "If it will really help her . . ."

"I promise," Dr. Clemens, the psychologist, intoned. "She'll be like a different child soon. You'll see."

Lisa is little for her age. She's eight years old. She has a head of boisterous, dark curls and big black eyes that she got from her father. She is simultaneously willful and fragile. In this, she is not like me, not like I was: a healthy, heavy, dumpling of a child, blonde and freckled. Even when her dad was here she cried easily, held on to hurt in a way that made me worried for her future happiness.

At the facility, which was a big, corrugated-metal building in a business park out in the suburbs, she was nervous, fidgeting and chewing on her hair. She held on to my pant leg as I signed us in at the front desk. She had been excited when I told her we were going to get her a Companion, but now she seemed so timid I began to wonder if this was a good idea.

"Don't worry, sweetheart," I told her as we sat in the waiting room, listening for our names to be called. "There's nothing to be scared of here."

"But what if I can't choose?" she said. "What if I don't know which one I'm meant to choose?"

"You'll know it when you see it," I said. "And if you really can't decide, we'll come back another time."

After a few minutes, a woman employee in nurse's scrubs called our names and introduced herself as Gretchen. She led us down a carpeted corridor into the windowless interior of the building. She spoke to Lisa in that cloying voice some adults use with children and that Lisa doesn't like. She explained that we were going to a room where there were "a whole bunch of special friends, who are all very excited to meet you and play with you." There would be other children there, too, but no grown-ups were allowed. She said this like it would be a special treat, but I felt Lisa grip my hand tighter when she heard it.

"I won't be far away," I said to reassure her.

No, Gretchen agreed, Lisa's mommy would be just outside, waiting for her while she decided which Companion she liked most of all and wanted to take home with her. Wasn't it great that she could take one of them home? Wasn't that the best?

"We think it's better for them to make the selection by themselves," she said to me. "That way she doesn't need to worry about pleasing you." I told her I understood.

I was relieved when Lisa let go of my hand, reluctantly but without tears, and went with Gretchen to the playroom. I went to the viewing room next door. It was small, low-lit, with a long, glass panel on one wall and a few chairs set up in front of it as if it were a movie screen. When I entered, there were several other parents there already. There was coffee on a counter, so I poured myself a cup, then joined the others peering through the glass.

The room beyond was cavernous, fluorescent-lit and over bright. Its walls were painted with flowers, trees and animals in garish colors. There were a few child-sized chairs, no other furniture, carpet wall-to-wall. Five or six children aged variously between four and ten stood or sat in different parts of it and around them flocked and flew, loped and crawled, an incredible variety of artificial animals. There were the ones that you'd expect: cats and dogs, hamsters, mice and guinea pigs, some birds with ice-cream-colored plumage, orange and magenta, pale pink and lime green. Then there were others, more surprising: a pig, a couple of iguanas lounging in a corner. There were some that had no analog in life but combined characteristics from different species: fat, waddling, fluffy things that looked half-toad, half-teddy bear; winged lizards with the hairy faces of friendly dogs.

I watched Lisa go among them. She stopped to pet a purple-and-white splotched rabbit with lopsided ears. Then she got distracted by the movement of an enormous butterfly that was the size of one of those old paperback books they used to publish when I was a child. She followed its meanderings across the room, reaching up toward it until, to her delight, it landed on her outstretched hand. It was ice blue with pink stars at the center of each wing. I watched her with it and thought how marvelous it would be to have something like that around the house, to come into a room and find it lighted on the wall, to see it perched on Lisa's hand or shoulder, a wonderful, flying jewel.

But then, as she was admiring the butterfly, something came toward her on the floor, a shape like a big, gray, bony hand. For a moment I was not sure what it could be. Then I felt a squirm of recognition. It was much bigger than the real ones that I sometimes find in our bathtub. When I was married, I would call Lisa's father in to deal with them because I can't bear to actually touch them. Now I try to wash them down the drain or catch them under a glass, then slide a piece of paper underneath and flush them down the toilet. I wondered why on earth the company would make a thing like that. What kind of child would choose *that* instead of something beautiful and soft?

I watched Lisa watch the scrambling collection of legs with sudden, rapt attention. I saw her shake the butterfly from her hand. It flew away chaotically across the room. She crouched down and put her hands out in front of the enormous spider, and waited. It hesitated for a moment. Then it scuttled forward and climbed onto her palms. She lifted it up and for a long moment looked into its face. (Is it possible to say that? Does it actually have a face?) After a minute, I realized that her lips were moving; she was speaking to it. What was she saying? I wanted desperately to know.

She let it crawl up her arm until it was on her shoulder. The children had been told that, once they had made their choice, they should come back to the door they'd entered by and wait. Lisa crossed the room and waited by the door. I could see that she was standing calm and still; all her anxious fidgeting from earlier was gone. Gretchen came and opened the door and Lisa smiled up at her and reached out to take her hand.

Spider, which is what she named her new Companion, rode on her shoulder all the way back home.

It is roughly the circumference of a salad plate with a dark walnut head attached to its bulbous abdomen. It is the same reflective almost-black as pencil lead; light slips over its exoskeleton when it moves across a room. Arched legs like jointed knives, a pair of tooth-shaped pincers where its mouth should be, a quartet of eyes. The eyes are domed, the dense and glossy dark of tinted glass, but somewhere behind each a curl of red light wriggles, shimmers, scans across the world.

I don't know much of how it works, what information the eyes absorb. Does it see the way we do, in light and color? Does it see in infrared, heat and movement? And where do those images go, how are they processed, how are they used? In some ways it acts more like a dog than like the living thing it's built to imitate. It follows Lisa everywhere. It seems to know its name and when it's being talked about. It will come when Lisa calls it and go when she sends it away. Beyond that, I'm not sure how intelligent it is. I tell myself that it is only a computer like any other, a machine, programmed by people for a certain function. But it is difficult not to attribute to it animal presence, sentience, emotion, strategy.

When it walks, its feet and joints make small, soft, clicking sounds, a rattling whisper like wind stirring dry leaves. Though it has lived with us now for months—no, that isn't right, it doesn't live—when I hear that sound, for a moment I still think I have left a door or window open. I look up. I see that it is just the spider, making its way across the floor or up a wall, taking its thousands of tiny mechanized steps.

I did not ever like having it around. But for a while it really seemed to work . Lisa started sleeping better with Spider curled beside her on her pillow. She stopped asking when her father would come back. During the day she was much calmer. Her fits of rage became less frequent, then stopped altogether. She has become, in fact, suddenly quite grown-up and independent for her age: some mornings she will dress and get ready for school all by herself; some evenings she will clear the dinner dishes and put them in the dishwasher without my asking her; and sometimes, recently, she'll even go up to bed all by herself, leaving me to get on with the work I didn't get done during the day.

True, we have had some arguments about whether Spider can be at the dinner table with us. I have insisted that he go into her room while we are eating. Dr. Clemens suggested that it would be helpful for me to set some boundaries like this.

And I do not like it when Lisa whispers to her spider so that I can't make out what she is saying. Sometimes it sounds to me like they are speaking in some language I do not even recognize, much less understand.

And, when it first arrived, I would be sitting reading late at night and I'd look up and see it standing on the wall across from me, perfectly still, eyes glittering. I learned to close my bedroom door at night after this happened a few times.

But in general, Lisa's companion seemed to be working just the way it should. Or at least it did until just a few weeks ago, when suddenly things started to go wrong and strange at once. It was on a Tuesday, I am pretty sure, yes, a Tuesday evening. That is when I found the web.

I had come home early from work that day, weary and frustrated as I usually am. I am a paralegal for a company downtown and I do not love my job. The lawyer I work for sometimes treats me like a secretary. She tells me to get coffee and make copies, and there's not much I can do except comply; I can't afford to lose this job now that I'm on my own.

I closed the front door after me, and the house wrapped me in its gentle quiet. Lisa was at her friend Kadesha's house that afternoon and therefore so was Spider. For once, I had the place entirely to myself. I sat down at the kitchen table and was going through the mail when I heard, from upstairs, a sound I couldn't understand: a soft but certain flapping like somebody was shaking out a bed sheet. I listened and it came again: a noise like a sail filling with wind. Was there a burglar up there making the beds?

I went upstairs and walked along the corridor looking in

each room until I came to Lisa's. The door was shut, so I pushed it open and went in. The room was arranged just as always: bookshelves and chest of drawers against one wall, bed against the opposite, the row of stuffed animals along the windowsill between. But as I looked I saw that over everything was a layer of thin, diaphanous threads connecting all the objects like a net. The threads were translucent and barely visible, but when I took a step inside I found that they were all around me, clinging to my skin and clothes. I stopped and tried to shake them loose, but they were sticky and would not come off. In the slanting afternoon light, they were silver, shimmering, and I could see that they all led toward one corner where they spiraled up into a dense silky canopy right over Lisa's bed. It was billowing gently in the light breeze that came in through the open window; this was what I had heard from downstairs.

I stared around me, partly entranced and partly horrified. How long had the web been there? Why hadn't Lisa told me about it? I felt a surge of anger, a feeling of betrayal. She had kept it secret. She knew I wouldn't like it and she was protecting her Spider by hiding it from me. But then I thought: why hadn't I seen it for myself? I tried to think of when I was last in my daughter's room and, with a lurch of shame, I realized that it had been several days, almost a week. How was that possible? Lisa had become so self-sufficient, not even needing me to tuck her in at night. And I had been glad to let her take herself upstairs, to look in on her later and see that she was sleeping peacefully; in the small glow of the nightlight I had not noticed all the fibers that were crisscrossing her room . . .

I went downstairs and got a broom out of the closet. I came back and, brandishing it in front of me, began to try to sweep away the strands. Where there were just a few, they snapped and cleared away. But where they were denser they were strong, and in the corner over Lisa's bed the broom got stuck. I pulled it but I could not get it loose.

It dawned on me how strange it was that until now Spider had not made a web. Why would it start all of sudden like this? I left the broom where it was and went down to get my tablet from my purse. I pulled up the owner's manual for Spider on the site of the company that had manufactured it. I looked through the manual, but it said nothing about web-spinning, only that in the event of any malfunctioning you should bring your companion back to the facility where you got it as soon as possible.

This was a malfunction. Wasn't it? It definitely was, and therefore Spider would have to go back to the facility. I remember that I stood there in the middle of my living room and almost whooped with unexpected joy. I had not known until then just how much I wanted to get rid of Spider. A strange thought came to me that Spider knew perfectly well how much I disliked it, that it had watched me and perhaps tried to find ways to keep me at a distance from my daughter so that she would keep it safe from me. But then I thought how ridiculous and paranoid that would sound to someone else. What had it done all these months except what it was meant to do?

As soon as possible, the manual said. That meant I'd have to break the news to Lisa when she got home. She would be upset of course. She would not like the prospect of letting Spider go. But what else could we do? We could not have it covering our house in a net of sticky threads. That would not be safe. I would tell her gently, calm but firm, and then we would drive together in the morning to the facility and she could pick out a replacement, a dog or gerbil or maybe that nice butterfly. I could already feel the contentment I would experience during that ride home, the sense that I was taking charge the way a parent is supposed to do. Lisa might not like it right away, but she would come to understand eventually that what I'd done was for the best.

Why had I lived for so long in a situation that made me so uncomfortable? At that moment, it seemed inexplicable.

I put the manual away and started thinking about dinner. I'd make one of Lisa's favorites, macaroni-cheese maybe, which might make her less unhappy when I told her that Spider had to go away. I started taking ingredients out of the cupboard, mixing and combining them, as I waited for my daughter and her spider to come home.

It must have been an hour or so later that the doorbell rang to let me know my girl was home. I went to get the door, looked outside, waved to Kadesha's mother, who was sitting in her car. She waved back then drove away as Lisa came inside.

There was Spider on her shoulder, with its legs folded together so it looked even more like a strange inhuman hand than usual. Lisa was in a happy mood. She had spent a lovely afternoon at the playground in the park. She twirled into the living room, telling me about how they fed the ducks, got ice cream, played on the swings and on the slide. She was cheerful all through dinner, sent Spider up to her room without being asked, cleaned her plate and even ate her broccoli. I gave her ice cream for dessert and waited until she had almost finished it before I cleared my throat and said:

"Lisa, sweetheart, there's something that I have to talk to you about."

She looked up at me with her enormous, lovely eyes and I thought I saw a flicker of alarm pass through them, but I might have just imagined that.

"I saw what Spider did up in your room," I said.

"Oh," she said. She looked down at her plate.

"I'm not mad at you because you didn't tell me about it, although you probably should have told me. But we can't have Spider making that kind of mess inside the house. It's not okay."

"But I like it," Lisa said. "Spider made it especially for me. He can take it down if I ask him to. And he promises he won't do it again . . ."

"Sweetheart, even if he did promise not to do it again, Spider isn't supposed to make a web at all. It means there's something wrong with him. Like he's sick and needs to go to the hospital. We're going to take him back to the place where we got him so that they can make him better."

Lisa looked stricken, a deer caught in the headlights of a car.

"Spider has to go away?" she asked.

"Yes," I said. "Perhaps not forever. But for a while at least."

I saw my daughter flinch and her eyes darted upward in

the direction of her room where Spider was. Then she looked back at me. In her expression, there was something I'd never seen before. Her eyes were narrowed like she was angry but also like she was suspicious, like I was someone she had to watch out for. It was a look that I'd seen a few times on her father when I started to find out about the secrets he had kept from me, the money he had used without my knowing, the late-night phone calls to a number that I didn't recognize. But I'd never seen it on my daughter until now.

"Mama," she said, "you don't like my Spider do you?"

Don't lie, I told myself. "No, sweetheart. I don't really like him much."

"What did Spider ever do to you?" she said.

"Nothing. It's just . . ."

"You can't," Lisa interrupted. "You can't take him away!"

In her voice I heard the rising swirl of panic, the trembling frantic sound that used to come before she went into full-fledged hysterics. I had not heard it in the last few months. I could see that her shoulders had gone rigid and her fists were clenched down by her sides. In a moment, I thought the tears would start gusting through her like a storm. But then, instead, she stood up from the table and ran upstairs.

I let her go. I sat and listened to her small footsteps climbing the stairs, then pattering down the hall. I heard the door of her room open and slam closed. All right, I thought, I'll leave her for a few minutes, let her cry . Then I can go upstairs and try to talk to her again. I cleared away her bowl of melting ice cream. I started the dishwasher. A strange feeling came over me and I realized that of course Spider was up there in her room, perhaps waiting at the center of its web over her bed. I felt suddenly on edge, though I could not have said exactly why. I listened for the sound of sobbing, any sound that might be coming from upstairs. But I heard absolutely nothing.

I climbed the stairs two at a time and strode down the hallway. I banged on Lisa's door and called her name. No reply came and so I pushed the door. It moved an inch or so, but then it stopped and would not open any farther.

Through the gap between the door and the frame I could see a thick crosshatch of sticky, pallid threads so dense they were preventing it from opening.

I called my daughter's name again. I pushed against the door and it moved this time, but only a few inches. I got scissors and tried to cut the threads but the scissors just got stuck. All the time, I called to Lisa and heard nothing in reply.

Finally, exhausted, I sat down on the floor. I thought: I'll call the fire department, the police. They'll know what to do. I stood up and was about to go downstairs to get the phone when I heard, quite close to me on the far side of the door, Lisa's voice.

"Mama," she said. "Mama?" She sounded small and young. I came and put my face against the door to get as close to her as possible.

"Lisa, sweetheart. I'm right here. Are you okay?"

"Yes, Mama, I'm okay."

"I'm going to call the firemen to come and get you out," I said.

She was silent for a moment. Then she said: "No, mama. Don't do that."

"But we have to get you out of there."

"You don't have to call the firemen. Spider can fix the door," she said. "He didn't mean to make it not open. He was just making more webs to cheer me up."

"Well, in that case, tell Spider to make it open right now."

There was quiet for a moment and inside the quiet, the sound of whispering.

"He doesn't want to do it," Lisa said, "unless you promise . . ." She trailed off.

"What? Unless I promise what?"

"All you have to do is promise that he doesn't have to go away. He can stay with us forever."

"Sweetheart, I don't know if . . ."

"Mama, please!" I thought she sounded suddenly afraid. "Just say that he can stay."

What could I do? "All right. Your Spider doesn't have to go away."

"Promise?"

"Yes, I promise," I replied.

On the far side of the door I heard what sounded like somebody snickering with mean, dry laughter, but as I listened more I realized that it was the sound of many legs moving back and forth across the wooden surface. What was it doing? I could picture it: scuttling this way and that, gathering the threads up and consuming them, taking them back into its gut, material to be stored for later use. Finally the door swung open. Spider scuttled over and perched on the windowsill. Lisa was sitting on her bed looking little and bereft. I gathered her into my arms and hugged her and she hugged me back, but not with the enthusiasm or relief that

I'd anticipated. She pulled away after a moment. I looked at her and now, instead of seeming young, she looked very old and tired.

"Why did you get so scared, Mama?" she asked. "My Spider would never do anything bad to me." She sighed. "If you want to take him back to where he came from, that's okay I guess."

I looked at her astonished. She sounded so sad that suddenly I could not bear to do it, not that night anyway.

"All right," I said, "but not today. We've all been through enough already."

That night I woke to find myself swaddled in a pale and sticky substance that made it difficult to move or breathe. I struggled to free myself but the more I struggled, the more tightly bound I got. Something was moving above me in the dark, back and forth, but I could not see well enough to know for certain what it was. I panicked and woke myself for real this time and found that it was morning. Light was slanting in between the blinds. Everything in the room was as it had been when I went to bed.

As I lay in bed, I decided what I was going to do: the next time that I found Spider on its own, when Lisa left it by itself at home or when it crawled out of her room one night, I would drop something heavy on it, a cast-iron pan or our big dictionary. I thought with satisfaction about the crunching sound its shell would make when it collapsed, the sight of it, cracked and broken on the ground, looking finally like the machine it always was.

That would be expensive, though. Since Companions are

leased monthly, I would have to give the full cost back to the company, which would mean we could probably not get a replacement. It was going to be difficult enough helping Lisa to adjust to Spider's loss. Maybe, instead of breaking it, I could just trap it underneath a mixing bowl and take it back undamaged. That should not be so difficult, I thought. I could buy one of those cardboard pet carriers to use to take it back to the facility.

That was now three weeks ago—or is it four? I am still waiting to carry out my plan. Lisa has been keeping Spider close to her a lot. There have been a few times when I thought I could catch it, but each time there has been some reason that I hesitated too long and lost my chance: Lisa had a bad day at school the day before and I wondered if this was quite the right time; it was late at night and the noise might wake the neighbors. But I will do it sometime very soon. I just have to wait for the right moment.

Through these past few weeks, Lisa hasn't spoken to me much. It's not that she's been sulking or obviously upset. She kisses me goodbye when I drop her off at school, she kisses me goodnight. She helps around the house. She is the same polite and placid child she's been since we first got her spider. But there is something perfunctory about the way she treats me, something dry, like it would not make much difference to her if one day I went away and did not return. Or at least, I think there is. Sometimes I find myself watching her and she seems to be unnaturally still, as if she has learned from her spider the art of infinite patience. I had a dream in which I saw her walking on all fours, her legs and arms arched up in angles that would be impossible for a human child, so she could scuttle forward at a rapid speed.

Since that one occasion, Spider has not made another web, at least not one that I've found. It is as if it learned its lesson, although I don't think it can learn. It acts exactly like it did before, and in fact there are times when I wonder what it would be like if I did nothing at all and we went on the way we are. Of course, I cannot let that happen. Sooner or later I will have to act. But there are evenings when I'm reading a bedtime story to my daughter and she is leaning against me and Spider is perched up on the wall above her bed and I forget that I am planning to get rid of it. For a moment, it is almost comforting to have another . . . I was about to use the word "person" but that does not make any sense. It is almost comforting to have another—what? Another some-one in the room.

If You Cannot Go to Sleep

First, she tries counting. The numbers move sluggishly through her head in single file like people in a line at the post office or at the bank or at the discount supermarket where you can only pay with cash so the line is always long and she is always frustrated by the time she reaches the counter and so, to compensate, she always tries to be extra friendly to the cashier, to be sure to instruct him or her to have a nice day after he or she gives back her change, because it seems worse, somehow, to be a cashier in a discount supermarket than it would be to do the same job at a place that sold expensive, gourmet foods, although when she thinks about this now, so late at night she doesn't even want to look at the clock to find out the time, she thinks why would it make a difference whether you ran a cash register at a place where people are buying brie and figs and Ethiopian fair-trade coffee or a place where people are buying Pampers and Wonder Bread? In reality, she thinks, working at the gourmet market is probably worse because of the annoying people who shop there, the men and women in stylish business-casual clothing, or athletic wear because they are coming from or going to the gym, all of them buying organic heirloom tomatoes and the latest variety of ancient grain that is supposed to make you live forever and exuding an air of self-satisfaction, of superiority, of knowing that they are worthy and admirable and enlightened beyond ordinary mortals, and wanting to chat with the cashier about his or her day and about the food they are buying and the fabulous, complicated meal that they are going to make with these ingredients, which is really just another way of showing off when you get right down to it. Do you really want to see those people every day? On the other hand, at the discount supermarket you might see people buying weird, sad, lonely food like the man who'd been in front of her in line the other week who was severely overweight and buying twenty frozen dinners for himself and nothing else, or else the unnaturally skinny woman buying a big crate of caffeine-free diet soda and nothing else, or else the mother with three children trying to figure out what she could afford with her WIC voucher, carefully watching the total as it came up on the screen, putting aside the things in her cart she could not manage to afford that week. For a cashier, that had to be depressing. Add to that the threat that any day now you will be replaced with one of those automatic swiper machines that don't really work and always require the customer to be assisted before he or she can check out, and you have a pretty unhappy work environment as a cashier one way or another.

Or maybe she is just being a snob and really being a cashier can be a fine job and only because of her particular, privileged background would she assume that it would be miserable to be a cashier, rather than fulfilling, because how does she know? The closest she ever came was waiting tables at a restaurant when she was in high school and that job was not terrible, she still has some good memories of the characters she met among the customers: the man who came up to the counter and asked her if she could recite any Shakespeare and she spoke aloud the prologue to *Henry V* because she knew it by heart, or the time she . . . well, actually that is her only good memory of that job, the rest of it was boring or unpleasant and involved mopping floors and stacking dishes and wiping down tables and laying traps for cockroaches and anyway she knew that she was soon going to go away to college and that this wouldn't be her job for the rest of her life, she would be able to leave and go to something better or at the time she thought it would be better. She did go to college and she majored in French and lived in Paris for a few years after she finished her degree and now she works translating technical manuals and she used to be married to a man who appeared to be steady and reliable if a little dull, qualities that she told herself were a good antidote to her own tendency to fret too much about small and insignificant things, and who had a successful career in hospital administration but who decided suddenly, about six months ago, that he'd had enough of expending his energy and intelligence working in a health-care system organized for the benefit of for-profit insurance companies and decided to move to France. She found this moderately ironic since, when she had been yearning a few years previously to ditch everything and go back to Paris, he had insisted that they could not do this because he'd put too much time and effort into developing his career in the United States and he did not want to throw away what he'd worked so hard to build. She pointed this irony out to him during the brief period after he'd announced that he was moving out but before he had actually departed for good, and although he readily agreed with her that, yes, there was some irony in his choice, he did not change his mind. He said that she worried too much and that he didn't want to deal with it anymore. And she said: this won't make me worry less. And he said: I know but it will no longer be my problem.

For the first few months after he was gone, she had seemed to be coping admirably; in fact she seemed to be adjusting to their separation astonishingly well, even to be calmer than she had been before he left. She told herself and her friends and her mother that perhaps it was for the best, they had never been perfectly matched after all, she had always longed for someone more expressive and exciting, who shared her love of literature and art, who longed to travel, who had a greater capacity for amazement. Perhaps this could be a new beginning and a chance to find a truly fulfilling life. She sold the house they had lived in together, rented an apartment within walking distance of a good coffee shop and a discount supermarket. She saw friends. She saw movies. She started taking a swing dance class.

But then, two days ago, as she was drifting off to sleep, her phone began to ring. Her mind surfaced from the soft, dark pool in which it had submerged, just in time to hear the last cycle of tones die away before her voicemail picked up. Her phone was in the kitchen and at first she thought that maybe she could burrow back down and find her way to the threshold of sleep again, but no, she was awake, wondering who had called so late. Her brain began to spin and gather speed. Could it be an emergency, something seriously wrong? A friend in trouble? Her mother in the hospital? She climbed out of bed and made her way down the hall and took the phone from the counter where she'd left it and stared at the string of digits on the screen. It was not a number that she recognized, but the country code was +33 and the numbers that followed were the area code for the town where, as far as she knew, her husband now resided. She knew no one else who might be calling her from there. Right now in western Europe it was early morning, well before dawn. She looked at the screen but there was no icon telling her anyone had left a message. She listened to her voicemail anyway, just in case. Nothing. She considered calling the number back but thought, suddenly, angrily, that she did not want to give him the satisfaction of having her jump to attention just because he dialed her number. Suppose he had not meant to call her at all; he'd only misdialed and that was why he hadn't left a message? Or what if he had meant to call her but then changed his mind? When he answered the phone his voice would be dry and distant and polite in that way he could be when he wanted to protect himself. She could not bear the idea of having him treat her coolly, so instead of calling him and asking him what he wanted, she put the phone back down on the counter and left it there and went and climbed back into bed. She lay down and clicked off the light on her nightstand. She closed her eyes and tried to go to sleep again. But she could not, and all that night, and the one after, and now again tonight, she has lain awake, staring into the dark, her mind like something stranded on a beach, longing to swim out and get lost at sea but unable to reach the water's edge.

Now, when she looks over toward the window, there is a blue glow seeping in beneath the blind. She does not know if she is angrier with her husband for calling her and unsettling her so much or with herself for allowing something as trivial as a phone call to make her come unhinged. She sighs. She looks over at the numbers on the alarm clock on the nightstand. Soon it will be time for her to get up. She might as well go and make some coffee and get ready to start work.

Since counting didn't work, the next night she tries imagining the sound of ocean waves. This is what it said to do on a website she found called Overcoming Insomnia when she should have been working on her most recent project, a book instructing engineers on the maintenance and repair of machines that shape the steel exteriors of cars and trucks on the assembly lines of the European subsidiaries of American car manufacturers. But she was too tired to concentrate and had drifted into looking online for answers to the question of what to do if you cannot get to sleep.

Imagining the sound of the sea seemed like a good exercise when she read about it, even though she is extremely suspicious of the whole idea that you can "overcome" insomnia, which sounds as if you are supposed to triumph by an act of will, wrestle your sleeplessness into submission, and which evokes intense concentration or brute force or both, when really what she needs is the exact opposite of this: a kind of soft dissolving of herself during which she turns from a person into a cloud of gold dust that hovers shimmering for a minute before dispersing into the dark with a sound like someone blowing out a candle. Insomnia is more like something you have to sneak under or find a hole in the fence of or find a way to flow around than something you can "overcome." Also, the man who produced the website, Howard Francus, MD, whose smiling photograph appears on many of its pages, has written a book with the same title as his website, *Overcoming Insomnia*, and the site is really a promotional platform for his book. She can't help suspecting that the information that Dr. Francus put on the website for free is only the peripheral stuff, the least effective and therefore least valuable insights and techniques he has to offer, because wouldn't he want to keep the really good stuff, the real secrets, the magic surefire answers to himself so that you had to buy his book? What would be the point of using the website to promote his book if everyone just read the website and was immediately cured and no one needed to pay $24.99 plus shipping and handling to find out how to go to sleep at night?

Nevertheless, in spite of her profound misgivings, lying in the dark, she tries to imagine the sound of the ocean. It has been a long time since she went to the ocean. As a child she used to live near the coast. Now she lives in a city that, although it is on a lake, is very far from the ocean. There are hundreds of miles of dry land in every direction. Before he left, she and her husband had been planning to go to the beach as soon as both of them could find time for a vacation. In fact, she loves the sea, the smell and sounds of it, the way it throws the light back up into the air so that all the objects near the shore, the houses and the people and the trees and the grass bowed over on the dunes, are tossed around inside a storm of light. How she misses the sea! And she and her husband never did get around to going there together because it always seemed like there was some reason to postpone the trip—either they needed to go and see his family or hers or there was some reason why he couldn't leave work or she had taken on too many projects to go away from home for an extended time—and so they delayed and delayed and sometimes when they were in bed at night and felt close to each other either because they had made love or just because some of the cold distance between them seemed to give way a little, they would talk again about going to the ocean, they would promise to make the time, they would get down the calendar and mark off a week and determine that the next day they would each do what was necessary to ensure that they could go away. But then something would come up and it wouldn't happen and after a while they stopped talking about it and then they stopped talking about anything at all.

At some point she realizes that she has said to herself that "they" felt close to each other and "they would determine" to finally take the time to spend together, but in fact she doesn't know whether it was only she who felt these things, the closeness and the renewed goodwill toward their marriage; she supposes that her husband shared these same emotions. But it is just as likely, given what happened later, that he was feeling and thinking something entirely different, although what it was she cannot know. He is a sealed box to her now, his mind and heart entirely opaque, and what is worse she understands that he always was this way; it only seemed that she could see inside him, all the way to the bottom of him as it is possible to see through shallow water at the edge of the sea.

Is she still concentrating on hearing the sound of the ocean, as Dr. Francus suggested? When she tries to call it back, all she can get her mind to produce is the grating sound of different kinds of engines, the hyperactive shrieking of a leaf blower or the nasal buzz of a lawn mower or the slicing, snorting sound of a motorcycle. Now the motorcycles multiply, there are many motorcycles all driving slowly through her head together. They rev their engines. There must be ten or twelve of them at least. She turns on the bedside light and fumbles on the floor for her glasses. The light coming out of the lamp is like a bouquet of knives. Is that too overwrought? How else to describe how piercing it is? It is made of levitating shards of glass. Tomorrow, if she still can't get to sleep, she will make an appointment to see her doctor and get some sleeping pills. She doesn't want to do this quite yet. Because what if the phone rings again, late at night, and she is too sound asleep and she misses it? Maybe she will give it just one more night before she gets the medication. Or maybe two.

The following night, she cannot get the idea out of her mind that someone is going to come into the apartment. She cannot picture the person's features, only his unusual height and bulk, which is masculine in a general way without taking on the concrete features of an individual man. He is not white or black, but he does appear to be wearing her father's favorite old cardigan, which was gray with round leather buttons and leather patches on the elbows. This is his only distinguishing characteristic. She doesn't know how he is going to get into her apartment. She has already checked that both doors and all the windows are locked. And yet, every time there is a noise close by, either from out in the street or from somewhere inside the building, she starts, convinced absolutely that it is the footsteps of this man. She can hear him coming down the corridor, approaching the door of her apartment. Now, somehow, he is inside her apartment. He is right outside her bedroom. He waits in the hall outside her door, until she has almost forgotten he is there and then he makes a noise.

She tells herself that there is no man, but the more she tries to convince herself of this, the more clearly she can picture him. His eyes are green and one is slightly higher than the other. His nose is flat and broad at the bottom, so he looks like a figure in a painting by Picasso. He does not appear to have a mouth at all, as though whoever made him forgot to give him one, but rather than being horrifying as you might imagine a person with no mouth to be, this gives him a quizzical kind of expression like he is listening with genuine curiosity, his head tilted slightly to one side.

What would she do, she wonders, if there really was a man outside her bedroom door? The door has a lock on it, but she does not usually lock it at night because there is no one else in the apartment and because she worries about what would happen if there was a fire in the middle of the night, whether if she locked her door it might not make it more difficult for her to escape or for the firemen to come in and rescue her. She has to balance the concern that someone might get into her bedroom with the concern that she might not be able to get out in an emergency. She imagines the fire chief shaking his head sadly as the local news reporters hold microphones out to him in front of the burned-out husk of her apartment building, and talking about how they managed to get everyone out except for one woman up on the seventh floor who had locked her bedroom door and they couldn't reach her in time. Asphyxiation, the fire chief says. People don't think about these things. Why would she lock her door like that? Was she worried about someone coming in? That is just ridiculous.

But is it so ridiculous? These things do happen, men breaking into women's homes and stealing things or assaulting them or worse. If she heard someone outside her door, what would she do? She could call 911 and hope they arrived fast enough to rescue her. She could try running out of her room suddenly, hoping to surprise the man so much that she would have a chance to get away, run out of her apartment, sound the alarm. She could try talking to the man, finding out what he wants, trying to appeal to his human side not to hurt her.

Outside her door, there is a sudden, loud, creaking sound, like the noise made by a stomping foot. He is right there. She sits up in the bed and turns on the light; the part of her that believes there really is someone in the apartment screams at her not to do this, that she has just given away her presence and now, surely, he will come in and—what? Kill her most likely. She tries to reason with herself. There is no one there. She needs to go out of her room and make certain of this. Maybe then she will be able to go back to bed and get some sleep.

She goes to the door. She takes a deep breath. She opens it, quickly, and sees that her hall is empty. But of course he could have withdrawn into another room, be hidden right now somewhere out of sight but watching her. She walks around her home, turning on the lights in each room, opening the closet doors. Soon the whole apartment is bright from end to end. She sits down at the kitchen table and remembers that when she would get scared like this in the past, which didn't happen very often, her husband would do what she herself has just now done. Walk through the house, turn on the lights, prove that there was no one hiding, no ghosts, no people, no one there but the two of them. Sometimes he would do it impatiently: stop being so silly. But sometimes he would do it gently, quietly, showing her the rooms with nothing in them to be frightened of. When he did this, she would calm down immediately. She would sleep happily and without interruption for the rest of the night. She would be aware of his body stretched beside hers in their bed, appreciative of its presence, because who else would have cared for her in this small, absurd way, even some of the time, except for him?

Now she sits down at the table in her dining room, with all the lights blazing around her, feeling extra bright as they do late at night. She puts her elbows on the table and her head in her hands. No one comes either to comfort her or to harm her. She is all alone.

She tries, in this order: valerian root tea, which makes her lose feeling in her tongue so then she is lying in bed awake with a numb tongue in her mouth that feels like something someone else left there promising to come back and get it at the end of the day but then forgot to do so; melatonin, which makes her more wide awake through the night so that even the fitful sleep she has been managing to get evaporates; a strange kind of herbal tea that she buys from a hippy herbalist store near her home that smells like armpit and looks a bit like armpit hair but that cannot, she tells herself, possibly be in any way really related to armpits. None of these things works. She keeps her phone in the same spot on the counter in her kitchen where it was when she got the first phone call from France, but it does not ring.

Then, one night, about a week later, she is lying in bed thinking about global warming. This is a topic that she has been returning to at night quite often, thinking about how the difficulty with trying to solve global warming is that anything you do, any effort human beings make, whether it is holding a conference or publishing a book or making a movie to try to spread the word and convince people that global warming is real, only adds to the problem. Almost everyone, in America at least, who goes to see the movie will have to drive a car to get there, or if they watch it at home, they'll watch it on a television that was made in China in a factory that uses fossil fuels and then sent to the United States on a freighter that also burns fossil fuels, and while they are watching the film they will be using electricity that also probably comes from fossil fuels. Similarly, if they hold a conference, all the people who travel there will have to fly and stay in hotels and use taxis. Basically, the only thing you can do that will have a positive effect on climate change, unless you are a scientist who is working to invent some brilliant alternative to gasoline and coal, is nothing. If you do nothing, travel nowhere, eat nothing, use no light and don't drive, you will not be contributing to the problem. Otherwise, you will be. Is there anything I do, she thinks, actually worth the damage that I cause just by being alive in this time and place? Really, the only time when we aren't damaging things is when we are asleep, in the dark in our beds, and now she doesn't appear to be able to do even that. Maybe it would be better not to exist, to disappear.

What if no one was able to sleep anymore? What if we created a world of such uncertainty and such loneliness that one by one everyone in America found that they were unable to fall asleep? Each one of us is awake in our separate apartments, which we don't share with anyone else because we didn't want to stay with our parents and we couldn't get along with our spouse and fewer of us than ever have children and even then, our children don't stay with us for very long. Each of us is wandering around our lit-up rooms, our minds scurrying down corridors like mice in a maze, unable to find our way to the soft place where we feel blessed, able to stop striving and allow ourselves to float along for a while on the currents of the world, which is so much bigger and more mysterious than we can imagine. Maybe we are lonely for a world that we do not and cannot understand, that swirls around us in a beautiful storm and for which we cannot be held responsible.

She realizes that she is falling asleep. She feels her body softening, her bed starting to sway gently like a boat on a lake. Her room is filling up, flooding, with a substance that looks like dark ink but that she knows will not drown her. It is up to the edge of her bed. Then it spills over, traveling down the channels in her sheets and bedspread, buoying her up so she starts to float away.

And then the phone rings. It slices through the softness of her dream with its hard, bright, electronic sound. She is not surprised to hear it, however; she has the sensation that she had been expecting it would ring just then, just at that moment. She gets out of bed and feels light and certain. The leaden haze of the last week, brought on by sleeplessness, has gone and her head is clear and her movements are sure and graceful. Even though she is just walking down the hall in her apartment she can feel the swish of her nightdress against her legs in a way that is pleasant and sensuous, her bare feet on the cool floor. She reaches the kitchen as the phone is on its third and final ring and she plucks it off the counter and answers it.

On the other end of the line, she can tell without him even speaking, is her husband. He says: "Don't worry. You don't need to disappear. Everything you do is valuable for its own sake. I love you and this love illuminates all that you do and everything about you. Even if I'm not there now, this is still true."

"How did you know that I was thinking about disappearing?" she asks.

"Because you are dreaming," he says. "Because this is a dream."

"Then I'm asleep?"

"That's right."

Of course this is a dream, she thinks. He is not really calling her. In real life he never used words or phrases about love and illumination. Strangely, though, she is not disappointed because she can feel the truth of what he has said, whether he really said it or not. She wants to hear him speak again, so she asks: "Will you always love me?"

"Yes," he says, "in a way I will. I will think of you every day of my life and often I will wish that I had not left. But that does not mean that I'll come back."

Again this seems right to her. She happens to glance down at her feet and it occurs to her that, since she is dreaming, she would like to float a little way above the floor, and so she does, feeling herself lift off the ground, her body growing weightless in the middle of the air. She is still holding the phone against her face, but she is no longer paying attention to her husband or what he might say next. She drifts toward the window of her living room, which is open although she knows that is not how she left it when she went to bed. Outside, there is the nighttime street, with its pools of light, the complicated maps the trees make against the sky. Her husband asks: “Do you miss me?” and she remembers that he is there, on the other end of the line. His voice sounds like an insect. If she reaches out, she can pull herself over the sill and swim out into the night. “I have to go,” she says. She puts the phone in the pocket of her nightgown.

And then she is away.

No-No

They are called to the meeting in the gymnasium by number. The Takagawa family, number 1205, cross the camp with the other families whose numbers start with 12. It is a cold, bright January day. The ground is caked with snow. Wind funnels down the valley from the north, blowing the snow up into white, ghostly wings.

When he looks back years later, Karl Takagawa will remember most vividly the constant wind. It is as if even the air is bored and restless, turning this way and that like an animal going crazy in its pen.

. . .

Other things will stay with him, too, fragments of memory clear and frozen as photographs: the fence that encloses the camp on all sides, the guard towers along its length, the armed sentries at the main gate, the little creek that comes in through a culvert nearby. In the summer the children waded in the creek, but for months it's been too cold. Now they all walk quickly, hugging their coats around them, to the looming, barnlike building where they've been told an important announcement will be made.

When they get to the gymnasium, the Center Manager is standing at the front of the room. He's a tall, broad-shouldered white man. He wears wire-rimmed glasses and a brown felt hat with a wide brim, which for some reason he keeps on indoors. This gives him the genial look of a scout leader or a park ranger.

The Center Manager waits until they are all seated. He looks around at the sea of faces. Then he coughs to clear his throat.

"You are being asked," he says—he uses this word, *asked*, as though they have some choice—"to fill out a questionnaire giving information about yourselves to the government. Once you've done this, you can apply to work or go to school away from here. To gain this privilege"—he uses this word, *privilege*—"you just have to answer the questions in a way that shows you are a loyal citizen of the United States. You'll have three days to complete the forms."

"Are there any questions? Raise your hands if you have questions."

No hands go up. There are, apparently, no questions.

While the Center Manager is speaking, two assistants walk around handing out the questionnaires. When they come to Leigh Takagawa, Karl's wife, they stop, confused because she isn't Japanese. Should they give her a form or not? They pass her by. They give forms to Karl's mother and father. They move on to the next family.

Karl reads over the form. It has twenty-eight questions and is three pages long. It asks if he is married and what his wife's race is. It asks where his parents were born, if he has siblings, what their names are. It asks whether he sends money regularly to foreign countries. It asks about his hobbies, what magazines he reads, where he went to school.

At the very end are the following two questions:

27. *Are you willing to serve in the armed forces of the United States wherever ordered?*
28. *Will you swear unqualified allegiance to the United States of America and faithfully defend the United States from any or all attack by foreign or domestic forces and forswear any form of allegiance to the Japanese emperor or any other foreign government, power or organization?*

• • •

Karl thinks to himself: *Now that we have you and your family locked up in a camp in the middle of nowhere, will you swear allegiance to the state that put them there? How about serving in our armed forces while your parents, wives and children are in jail for doing absolutely nothing? How does that strike you?* From inside his chest, where the anger and disappointment have taken up permanent residence, come answers clear and certain. Will he serve? Will he swear allegiance? No and no. The government can take its *privilege* and go to hell.

Karl arrived in the camp five months before, in September 1942. All Japanese had been ordered to leave the western coastal states. He accompanied his parents, leaving his wife and daughter, exempt from banishment, behind in San Francisco. He thought he might not see them until the war was over.

But Leigh followed him a few weeks later. During their one phone call after the evacuation, as it was called, Karl tried to tell her not to come. She and May should stay in the city. Their friends in the Party would give her money until she found a job. In wartime San Francisco there were jobs even for women, even for Reds.

Instead of countering what he said, Leigh simply asked: "Which books do you want me to bring?"

When he saw her step off the bus, holding May on her hip, he was seized with such emotion that for some minutes he found it difficult to speak.

They sleep in Building No. 147, a cabin with unfinished

walls and a tar-papered roof. They share its one room with Karl's parents and another family, the Shinedas. They've hung a sheet across the middle of the room for privacy. Mrs. Shineda is a nosy gossip, so this barrier seems insufficient but it is better than nothing.

They have two beds, and Karl built a table and chairs from scrap lumber begged from the camp authorities. At night, the wind comes through the gaps in the walls. It wakes up May, who sleeps between them. They have tried to fill the cracks with newspaper but it seems as if no matter how many crevices they stop, the wind always finds a new way in.

The evening after the questionnaires are handed out, Karl tells Leigh that he's going to answer *no* to the last two questions. His parents are still at the mess hall eating dinner. May is playing outside with other children who sleep nearby.

Leigh listens to him quietly.

"What do you think will happen if you answer *no*?" she asks when he's finished speaking.

"I don't know," he says. "All I know is that I can't just pledge allegiance and say I'll go into the army. Not after this."

Leigh thinks about this for a minute.

"I think you're right," she says. "The one thing that they can't take from you unless you let them is your conscience."

Leigh is a slight woman who is often mistaken for younger than her age; if you didn't know her you might think that she was weak and tractable.

"It's so stupid," she says. "You were ready to go before they sent us here."

This is true. During the months before evacuation, they had many conversations about Karl joining up. He'd wanted to do the right thing, to fight against the Fascists. He would probably be in the army now, except that he was sent here, to this camp, instead.

He reaches over to take Leigh's hand and they sit for a minute like this, looking at each other in the growing gloom.

Then, from behind the bed sheet curtain that divides the room comes the sound of footsteps. Karl looks over and sees, in the gap beneath the curtain, a pair of feet.

Mrs. Shineda has been on her side of the room the whole time they were talking. She has heard everything they said.

Mrs. Shineda's feet go over to the door and wiggle out of their house slippers. At the door, where the sheet ends and there's a gap, she looks toward them, bows slightly and smiles. *Itte kimasu,* she says. I go and I return. Then she steps out into the dusk.

"Oh, well," Leigh says. "People were bound to find out soon enough."

But Karl does not like it.

A Japanese expression comes into his head, one that he dislikes for being fatalistic: *shikata ga nai.* There's nothing to be done. It was what his mother said when they were ordered from their home. It was what his father said when he had to close his store and lay off his employees.

And now Karl will have to sit here while the news of his decision goes out into the world. *Shikata ga nai.*

The next morning, Karl is with his work detail.

Their group has been assigned to construct more sleeping cabins so each family in the camp can eventually have its own. In December there were riots over the crowding and the bad food and since then the administrators have embarked on an improvement plan. They employ internees for wages to make the camp more habitable.

Like Karl, who was a schoolteacher, the other men did different things before. One was a plumber, one worked in a cannery, one used to be a fisherman. Although it is against camp rules, they speak to one another in Japanese. In the cold air, their breath plumes. They talk about the questionnaire.

"I'm just going to answer the way they want," the ex-plumber says. He hammers down tarpaper at one corner of a roof, while the ex-fisherman holds his ladder steady. "*Yes* and *yes*. What else can we do?"

The others murmur in assent. Then the ex-plumber looks over to where Karl and the ex–cannery worker are kneeling on a tarpaulin, attaching hinges to a door. "Hey, Takagawa," he says. "I heard that you are going to say *no* and *no*. Is that true?"

"That's right," Karl says. He doesn't look up from the work he's doing, just keeps screwing in the hinges.

"Why?" the ex-plumber asks.

"Because I don't think it is right to force us to say we are loyal, or to make us go into the army when our families are here."

"You aren't loyal?" the ex-plumber asks.

"The point isn't whether I'm loyal or not," Karl says. "The point is they don't have the right to ask me. They are treating us like criminals when we've done nothing wrong."

The ex-plumber opens his mouth as if he's going to say something else, but then he shuts it again and just rolls his eyes.

The ex-fisherman shakes his head. He says: "I heard that if you say *no* to either question, they send you away. To a camp in Washington State."

"We're already in a camp," Karl says.

"That place is worse. Like a real prison. I mean, no hot water, prison rations. No movies, no sports teams. And no families allowed, just men."

"How do you know so much about it?" the ex–cannery worker asks.

"One of my cousins from Seattle got sent to that place for running away to go home and see his girl. I heard about it from my uncle. It's called Tule Lake."

Karl feels like he should say something, but what? It doesn't matter what the consequences are, he's made his choice. But he thinks that he won't mention this conversation to Leigh. No reason to worry her any more than he already has.

Near the end of their work shift, when the other two men are out of earshot, the ex–cannery worker, whose name is Fred Nakamura, turns to Karl and says quietly: "I wish I had the guts to do what you are doing," and Karl feels a surge of unexpected pride.

When Karl comes back from work that afternoon, he finds his father sitting at the table in Building No. 147.

"I don't know," he says when Karl enters. Karl sees the questionnaire forms spread out in front of him. "If I forswear allegiance to the Emperor of Japan, aren't I saying that I used to *have* allegiance to him? Is it some kind of trick question?"

Hisao Takagawa has a shock of white hair on the top of his narrow head. For twenty years he owned and ran a clothing store on Fillmore Street. Now the store is shuttered and the inventory sold to competitors for a fraction of its value.

"For you," Hisao goes on, "this is not so bad. You are a citizen, not even married to a Japanese. There's no chance they'll deport you."

"*Otōsan*," Karl says, "they aren't going to deport you."

Karl has always been impatient with his parents' nervous self-defensiveness, their reluctance to trust non-Japanese. Karl was born in California. His childhood memories are filled with San Francisco's bright and shifting light, its banks of silver fog and rows of pastel-colored houses. Their neighborhood was full of *Issei* and *Nissei*, speaking Japanese, eating the foods—*mikan* at new year, *sunamono*, *manju*—and playing the music of their old homeland. But he also remembers white people and black people and Chinese living only streets away.

Once or twice when he was a teenager, he was called *chink*

by white men in the street, older men with heavy faces and clothes more worn than his. He ignored them. Already he was interested in Communism, in the Party and its promise of a future where race and class and countries would be swept away. And where would this great change take place if not in America?

Hisao shrugs: *who knows?* He clears his throat. "I have heard," he says, "a rumor."

"That I am going to answer *no* to questions 27 and 28."

"Is it true?"

Karl nods and Hisao sits back and folds his hands over his knees. "Well," he says. "Please think about your mother and me before you make your answers. That is all I ask."

"*Otōsan,* my decision doesn't have anything to do with you. You won't be punished for what I do. It doesn't work like that."

"Is that right? How does it work if you know so much about it? Would you have thought that you could find yourself where you are today?"

Later that evening Karl is eating dinner in the mess hall, when out of the corner of his eye he sees someone enter the room and come toward him. He looks over and sees it is Keo Sasaki, followed by a couple of other men whose names he does not know.

Mr. Sasaki owned a big dry-goods store in his old life. There is talk that he ran a bookmaking operation, too, but no one knows for sure if this is true. Since evacuation, he has become the self-appointed spokesman for the internees, and a delegate to the Japanese American Citizens League from the camp. The administrators talk to Keo Sasaki if they want to know what people in the camp are thinking. Karl has heard him say that the American Japanese are fortunate that the government brought them to the relocation centers for their own protection, that it has provided them with work and schools and housing at a time of national crisis.

Now he comes to where Karl is sitting.

"Mr. Takagawa," he says. "Would you walk outside with me?"

They go slowly, making a circuit around the building. Mr. Sasaki takes cigarettes from the breast pocket of his coat and offers one to Karl who accepts it. He is not afraid of Keo Sasaki, he tells himself.

At last Mr. Sasaki says: "I heard something and I want to find out from you if it is true."

"What did you hear?" Karl asks. He knows the answer perfectly well, but to admit that would be to confirm the suspicion.

"You are going to refuse to swear your allegiance to our country." He takes a pull on his cigarette and exhales smoke.

"The way I answer those questions is no one's business but mine," Karl says.

Mr. Sasaki sighs. "I wish," he says, "that were true. I wish none of us had to answer any of these questions. We wouldn't be here at all. We'd be at home. Your father would be running his store, I would be running mine . . .

"Unfortunately, we are at war. Normal considerations

have to be suspended. Think about this for a minute. We have said to the authorities here and to the War Relocation Office that we shouldn't be imprisoned because we are loyal Americans. How will it look if, when they ask us, some of our young men refuse to pledge their loyalty?

"Don't you want to be allowed to leave this place? Think about the welfare of your people."

Karl feels the anger tighten in his face. "My people aren't only Japanese," he says. "I act in solidarity with anyone who tries to do what is right when other people try to convince them to do what is easy."

Mr. Sasaki stops walking. "Is that really what you think?" he says, wearily. "Have you looked around? I don't see very many of your non-Japanese brothers in this camp. I didn't see them protesting when we were sent away last year. On the contrary, I saw them lining up to buy your father's stock for nothing and live in your vacated apartment."

His voice has risen in anger, but now he resumes walking at his slow, meditative pace. "I understand you are a man of principle," he says. "Just remember that I am not the only one who knows what you mean to do. Other people might not be so tolerant, you know. People get angry, get frustrated and then who can say what could occur? I dislike the idea of anyone being hurt."

Mr. Sasaki drops the butt of his cigarette onto the frozen ground where it rolls and makes a black dash on the frost. Then he turns and walks away without another word.

Karl goes back to the mess hall to finish eating. No one asks him what Keo Sasaki said. Leigh takes May to get ready for bed and he stays at the table talking and smoking with a few men in the light and warmth.

As he is walking back to Building No. 147 he notices that he is being followed. There are three figures, maybe four walking behind him. Karl walks faster and so do they. He turns left down one of the rows of cabins. They turn left, too.

He stops and turns to face them. Now he counts five in all.

"What do you want?" he says loudly, hoping that people in the surrounding buildings will hear.

"Are you Karl Takagawa?" one figure asks.

"Yes," he says. He stands up straight. "What do you want?"

The one who spoke approaches and Karl recognizes him, a skinny kid with slicked-back hair, though he does not know his name.

"We wanted to tell you," the young man says, "that we are going to answer *no*. We've decided. Why should we go into the army now? We have to stand up for ourselves."

Karl looks around at the others for the first time. They are all nodding and in the near-dark he can see that they are smiling. He laughs out loud with relief and claps the slick-haired leader on the back.

"Well done," he says. "Well done. That's great. We'll show them."

But later, when Karl tells Leigh what Mr. Sasaki said to him, she sits down abruptly on their bed like someone has let go of the strings that were holding her upright.

"He's just a trumped-up old windbag," Karl says. "It doesn't mean anything."

Leigh says, "I heard that if you say *no* you might get sent away. To another camp. Is that true?"

"I don't know."

"But you heard about it, too?"

"Yes. I heard about it."

"And you didn't tell me?" He does not reply to this. Leigh looks away from him, and he can tell that she is trying not to cry.

That night Karl cannot sleep. Eventually he gets out of bed and feels his way across the room. By touch he finds his coat and cigarettes. He opens the door and steps outside. The only lights are the arc lamps on the guard towers and over the main gate.

He sits on the front stoop and smokes. After a minute, he hears the door creak open behind him. May is standing there.

"I can't sleep," she says. "I want to sit with you."

"All right, just for a minute." He opens one side of his coat and she curls against him.

"Daddy, why won't Doreen play with me?" May asks.

Oh, dear. Doreen is Keo Sasaki's niece. How can he explain this mess in terms a six-year-old can understand?

"Well," he starts, "Do you think that you should do what is right even if other people don't like it?"

"Yes," May says.

"So I made a decision that some people don't like."

"I see," May says. Her voice is sleepy. "I wish that Doreen would stop being mean to me."

"She will," he says, hoping he sounds like he is sure.

. . .

The next day, the last before the forms are due, everyone is subdued.

When Karl comes back to change his shirt before supper, he finds Leigh sitting on the front steps of Building No. 147 looking distraught.

"I can't find May. She didn't come back from school with the other kids."

He can tell that she's imagining the worst: an accident or some harm visited on May because of Karl. He goes to Leigh and takes her hand.

"Don't worry," he says. "She can't be far. You stay in case she comes back here. I'll go and find her."

He searches among the cabins. He calls May's name. He asks any children he meets if they've seen her. He knocks on the doors of the cabins where her playmates' families sleep. No one has seen her.

It is already beginning to get darker and colder. What if she has fallen and hurt herself? What if she is hiding, scared because of something the other children said or did?

Some of the people he asks come out to help him search. Hana Sumiyoshi puts on her husband's big overcoat since she does not have one of her own. Helen Nakamura, who works in the mess hall where they eat. The guys from his work detail, even the ex-plumber. Some of the children May plays with after school, some adults he doesn't know. Soon there is a big group of them hunting through the cabins altogether.

. . .

It feels like some kind of parade, some kind of celebration, all of them out with flashlights and hurricane lamps that shine gold in the gathering blue-gray dark. Still there is no sign of May.

Finally, a little boy tells him that he saw a girl and a boy going toward the main gate of the camp a short while before. Karl sets off in that direction.

As he comes in sight of the gate, he notices that both the sentries have left their posts, which is strange. He keeps going toward the edge of the camp, looking for some sign of the children. Then he sees where the sentries have gone. They are over where the little stream runs along the boundary fence, standing among the gray skeletons of bushes on its banks. It is almost completely dark now, but they are illuminated by the arc lamps that shine along the boundary fence to prevent escapes: two white men in mud-colored uniforms, long wool coats, wool hats under their helmets.

They are looking down at something in the ditch.

Karl is behind them, so he cannot see their faces, and they have not heard him approach; he is perhaps twenty-five feet from them, but the wind blows away the sound of his footsteps. He hesitates. He does not want to seem to have been sneaking up on them. They are armed, after all.

Then, while he is deciding what to do, he sees one of the sentries nudge the other with his elbow: *hey, watch this.* From the holster on his belt, the man draws out his pistol.

With a big exaggerated movement that uses his whole arm, he aims it at something in the stream bed in front of him, something Karl cannot see.

Karl stands rooted to the spot. His throat has gone dry. Is it an animal the man is aiming at? A tin can stuck in the ice? The man is still poised as if he's going to shoot, as if he's looking for just the right angle from which to fire.

After a little while, the other man seems to grow uncomfortable. He reaches over and pushes the barrel of the pistol down toward the ground. The first man laughs and holsters his gun. Then both men turn and walk back toward their posts at the main gate.

Karl, standing in the dark, watches them come toward him. He thinks that at any moment they might see him. But the darkness is full now and they pass by about fifteen feet from him without knowing it.

When they are gone, he approaches the place where they had stood. He looks down toward the stream. And he sees, as he expected, as he hoped he would not, the children.

In the spilled arc light, he can just make them out: May and a boy about her age. They are absorbed in looking at the great blue-white icicles that are hanging over the entrance to the culvert. They have noticed nothing.

May looks around when she hears his footsteps coming down the bank. Her eyes are wide in the dimming light. Karl grabs her by the hand, yanks her around to face him.

"Don't you ever, ever run off like that again," he says.

He takes both children by the hand and marches them up the bank and back across the snowfield to where they sleep.

Leigh sends the boy, Ken Ozu, back to his family and puts May to bed early as punishment. She cries herself to sleep and they sit there listening to her cry, talking in whispers.

"Where did she go?" Leigh asks.

"She was looking at the icicles." Karl sees again the children at the culvert mouth, the guards. He takes a breath and when he lets it out, it is a sob.

Leigh looks at him.

"What's wrong?" she asks.

For a moment he considers telling her. But what good would that do? Later, he thinks, later, when they are no longer in the camp, when they are somewhere far away.

"I'm fine," he says. "Just tired. Just . . ." He does not know what to say next.

She looks at him like she doesn't quite believe him.

"Well, let's go to bed," she says. And so they do.

In the end, he does not tell her. In fact, he tells no one until many decades later when a PhD student from Berkeley called Julie Chen asks him for an interview. Leigh is four years dead by then, from cancer, and the young woman seems friendly, earnest. She reminds him of May when she was a student, before she moved to Michigan and started her own family. He is not sure why, finally, he decides to speak of what he saw, but once he starts it feels like he's been waiting all this time to tell it.

. . .

When he's finished, Julie Chen sits silent.

"You never told anyone this before?" she asks at last. Karl shakes his head.

"I never told."

"Why not?"

"I was afraid. Until then I did not know that people could do that, make a joke of killing. I mean, I'd read about such things in the newspaper. But I must not have believed them. I think this is what I learned at that time. People are capable of any bad thing."

"Yes," Julie says. "I think I understand."

Karl looks at her: her lineless face, her beautiful, well-made clothes. She has grown up in a time of nervous plenty. No, in spite of what she says, she doesn't really know what he is saying. He could try to tell her this, but it wouldn't do any good. Instead, he should just pray that she never learns to perceive her own unknowing.

"And what about the questionnaire?" Julie asks. "What did you decide to answer in the end?"

For a moment Karl, whose mind wanders off quite easily these days, hesitates.

"The . . . what?" he asks.

"The questionnaire. Did you answer *yes* or *no* to the last two questions?"

"Oh," he says, "I answered *yes* and *yes*. Then I applied to work outside the camp so I could take my family away from there. We lived in Iowa for a while."

"What about the young men who answered *no* and *no* because of you? What happened to them?"

"They were sent to Tule Lake or other places like that."

"You must feel pretty bad about that . . ." Julie Chen says. "You encouraged them but they were the ones who got in trouble."

"No," Karl says. "I don't feel bad. You see, I answered *yes* and *yes* and I was allowed to leave the camp. But the young men, the ones that had no wives or children yet, it was different for them. The ones who answered *yes* and *yes*, they were conscripted to the army. They were sent to Europe to fight. They were given very dangerous missions. Many of them were killed. But the no-no boys, as they were called: they had a hard time but at least they did not die."

"So something good came of it," Julie Chen says. Then she realizes how foolish this sounds. "I didn't mean . . ." she says. "I'm sorry."

Karl shrugs. He watches her as she makes her notes. Inside him, he can feel a swirl of white and cold begin, and hear the lowing sound of wind, even though the day outside is bright and still. Here are the pools of arc light; the gray hunch of mountains to the east. He's carried them around with him all this time. He can see again the man drawing his gun, aiming it. There is nothing he can do to stop it.

Guided Meditation

First, before we begin, find a comfortable position. You can be sitting in a chair or lying down on the floor or on a bed. You can be on your side or on your back or on your stomach. Whatever is right for you. Whatever you prefer.

Once you find your position, let your head rest easily and let your hands fall open. Allow your arms and legs to relax so that you can feel how they are supported by the surface beneath you. Release the muscles in your shoulders, your neck, your back. Relax your forehead. Let your breathing slow.

Is all this clear? Remember: this is about finding the pose that is right for your body. As long as you are comfortable, you can even stand up if you want. At least, I suppose you could, I don't see why not, although that would be kind of unusual. I don't want you to worry about it too much, and I certainly don't mean to imply that something as trivial as the position in which you decide to sit or lie will affect your ability to get the full range of benefits meditation can provide. That isn't how it works. I mean, do you really think that if there was someone who couldn't lie down or sit in a chair because of a disability, that he or she couldn't access his or her deeper states of consciousness? I think you should probably examine the prejudices that underlie that assumption as soon as you are finished meditating.

So whatever you would like: sit, stand, lie down. I suppose you could stand on your head if you wanted, although why you'd want to do that, I'm not sure. Once, I taught a guided meditation class at a local community center and there was a man who came every week, a young man with piercings and tattoos in Celtic-looking patterns all over his torso that you could see because he never wore a shirt in class, and who always arrived carrying the same courier bag covered with the logos of punk bands from the 1980s, bands that he could not possibly have been old enough to see live or even to have bought their music while they were still recording. Each week, while he was sitting on his mat waiting for the class to start, he would be smiling smugly to himself like he had discovered the secret stash of endorphins at the heart of existence, and then when class began and I would say that part about finding whatever position suits you best, he would—this is really true—flip up into a shoulder stand and stay like that the entire time.

Can you imagine how distracting that was for the other

students? For me? I mean, he could not have found a better way to call attention to himself if he'd stood at the center of the room screaming "Look at me!" over and over. At least if he'd screamed, I could have asked him to leave but as it was I couldn't really say anything because, after all, I had just told everyone that they were free to take any posture they wanted and I didn't want to seem to have suddenly turned judgmental and hypocritical.

Every week, when time for class rolled around again, I'd hope that maybe he wouldn't come, but he always did, regular as clockwork. Eventually, he started to unnerve the other students so much that the numbers in the class dropped drastically and the community center canceled it and filled that timeslot with Jazzercise instead. I lost my job, which was really terrible for a while, although I'm over it now that I've started making these recordings. All because of Mr. Shoulder Stand. Wherever he is now, I hope that one day he's doing a shoulder stand and his neck gets stuck so his head is permanently frozen at a 30-degree angle to his shoulders and for the rest of his life he has to walk around looking at his own belly button. That would serve him right.

Anyway, once you are in your comfortable position, whatever it might be, close your eyes. Relax your eyelids. Feel your tension ebb away. Feel it draining down, as if it was water being let out of a sink, slowly spiraling toward the drain until it is gone. If you don't feel the tension draining out of you, you really need to try a bit harder to relax. And don't tell me that you don't have very much tension to get rid of, because obviously you do. Otherwise why would you be doing this meditation? If you were just fine, if you had no stress or problems, you'd be out doing something more productive with your time, like brushing up on your Spanish or finally learning how to ballroom dance or volunteering to help the hungry or the homeless or some other group of needy citizens in your community. Or you might be reading one of those books that you still haven't read even though it has been on your list of must-reads for years now, like *War and Peace.* But instead you are here lying or sitting or squatting or whatever because at some point you felt bad enough and tense enough to buy this recording.

I don't claim to know what your particular problem is, of course. Maybe you have trouble getting to sleep. Or else you have trouble staying asleep through the night. You wake up in the early morning hours, in those dead-still hours before dawn when even the stray cats are silent, and you find your heart racing and your stomach doing flips inside you, and you are certain that there is some all-important thing that you forgot to do the day before and, though now you can't remember what it was, you're just as certain that your failure to do this forgotten, all-important thing will alter your life forever, irremediably, for the worse, and you lie in the dark with your heart flailing in your chest like a drowning person until finally after what seems like years dawn comes seeping underneath your blinds in a sad flood.

Or maybe that isn't it at all. Maybe, instead of being anxious, you're depressed. Maybe each day you drag yourself from bed feeling like someone has been scraping out the inside of your skull with a spoon the way that people scrape the rinds of their breakfast grapefruits. Maybe, as you move robotically through the hollow morning rituals of making coffee, showering, brushing your teeth, going to work, you feel like all you want is to crawl back into bed to hide. Maybe your bones feel like they are made of lead. Maybe you drink every afternoon at five to try to relieve the tightness in your throat that feels like a hand clamped around it, squeezing and squeezing without stint.

Maybe you felt some or all of these things when you picked out this recording in the bookstore or clicked to purchase it online. I don't know what made you so desperate for the calm and insight meditation brings that you decided to make that purchase. I would never claim to know that. I'm not you.

But, whatever it was, this is really, really not the time to be thinking about those things. How do you expect to be able to enter into a state of mind to gain perspective on your life when you are so wrapped up in thinking about how bad you feel? You really have to let it go, at least temporarily, if you want to move forward on this spiritual journey. Do you really think that your problems are going to go anywhere if you stop paying attention to them for a while? I can tell you from experience: they will not. They will still be waiting for you when you open your eyes. So, for god's sake, let it go for just a little while.

I mean, think about me for a second. I have put a lot of effort into making this recording, developing this whole experience for you and you can't even be bothered to pay attention to it for the time it takes to complete it. In all seriousness, show me the respect of trying to follow my instructions. Or if you can't do that, at least pretend, so that I don't have to feel any worse than I already do. That shouldn't be so much to ask.

Okay. Now you are relaxed. All your tension has melted away. You feel like you are floating, your body light and soft, your mind relaxed but sharp and alert.

I want you to imagine that you are walking along a corridor. Any corridor in any kind of building will do, although it's probably better if it isn't one of those institutional corridors, the kind you find in high schools or underfunded public colleges, with linoleum tiles on the floor that alternate between cheese-color and pigeon-color and no windows and the cinderblock walls that look like someone chose their shade because the paint company had it on sale back in 1973 last time they decorated. I have spent quite a lot of time in corridors like that, and I'm telling you that some other kind of corridor will work better for this exercise. Like a corridor in an expensive hotel or a grand, old, Ivy League library or an exclusive Asian-style spa—someplace more reminiscent of wealth, comfort and attention to interior design.

Hospital corridors are not great for this either, for obvious reasons. Although of course, as always, it is up to you.

Walk down the corridor. At the end of the corridor is a set of elevator doors. Press the button to call the elevator. Naturally, the elevator doors will be part of your imaginary corridor, so if you failed to take my previous advice and you pictured a corridor in a DSS office or a halfway house, the door might have a dent or a curved black scuff mark where someone kicked it in frustration some time ago and no one has yet come to repair the damage. There might be graffiti on the door written in marker pen or scratched into the paint at just about eye level so that you more or less have to look at it while you wait. Maybe this graffiti is telling you the names of two people who plan to be 2gether 4ever. Or maybe it is someone's name scrawled in some stylish but unintelligible way. Or maybe it is obscene: pictures of human body parts or indictments of someone's virtue or fidelity or sexual prowess.

If you haven't pressed the button to call the elevator, you should hurry up and do so. The rest of us don't want to wait while you hang around looking at the drawing of breasts on the door of your imaginary elevator.

The elevator arrives and the doors open. You step inside. The elevator should be empty. I hope, for your sake, it is. If there is someone in the elevator, you might want to think seriously about not getting inside because that is not part of this meditation. I can't tell you who this person in the elevator is or what they are doing there. This is not my imaginary elevator, it is yours.

Perhaps the person in the elevator is someone you knew a long time ago and are pleased to see. Like a childhood friend or an older relative whom you've missed very badly since her death. Or it could be someone you don't really care whether you see or not, your fifth grade math teacher or your mother's hairdresser. If it is one of those people, you can probably go ahead and get inside the elevator without fear.

But then again, perhaps it is a complete stranger, someone who doesn't seem quite right when you look at him. Maybe he's shaped strangely, as if his limbs had been stapled to one another after they were manufactured separately rather than growing altogether the way normal people do. When he moves, it might be in a disjointed, marionette way, one muscle at a time, so when he turns to look at you, he moves only his head, not his neck or body. You see his face in the dim, watery light of the single bulb stuck in the low ceiling and it looks like a cloth bag full of flour, white and ponderous; his eyes are nearly swallowed up by it. He is tall and broad and he is wearing an old leather jacket that is too small for him and that looks like he found it in the trash. His white T-shirt and jeans are covered with the dark blotches of grease stains the size of fingerprints. His hair is like the stubble after a field has burned.

Have the elevator doors slid closed yet? If they have not, you could wait for the next car, although who knows how long that will take, or you could just get in and ignore the person standing in the corner. It could be that he won't do anything, that he is just an unfortunately unattractive man with dirty clothes, someone who's had a hard time for reasons that you can't know. Your forebodings could very well be just your own shallow judgment based on his appearance. You'll have to make up your mind and get in the elevator to find out. Whatever you decide, could you consider doing it soon? It is time to go on to the next part of the exercise.

Have you stepped inside? Press the button to go down to the lowest floor. Watch the doors slide closed. Is there a man beside you in the car? Is the man watching you? Look over. Don't be too obvious about it, because if he does turn out to be a threat of some kind, you don't want to provoke him. The doors have just slid shut and now you are inside the elevator, trapped there until it gets to the bottom of the shaft and that could be a long time, depending on whether the elevator is fast or slow. If you imagined a corridor in a municipal government building or something like it, this is probably a slow elevator that takes whole minutes to go through each floor. I wish you had followed my advice and that you were in a Ritz-Carlton somewhere, but we'll just have to make the best of what you've created here.

It's descending now, you can feel that wobbly, lifted feeling you always feel when you ride in elevators. There are numbers on a panel by the door and you watch the lights blink as you pass each floor. The man beside you, if there is one, makes a noise that is somewhere between a grumble and a snort. It's possible he smells. Only you can know what the ingredients of that odor are and whether it is mild or strong, a faint whiff or a stench so powerful it starts to make your eyes water.

Don't blame me if that is happening. I didn't put the man into the elevator with you, you did. In fact, I told you to imagine the elevator was empty and then warned you not to get in the elevator if it was occupied. So this is not my fault. However, although it is not my fault, I will nevertheless try to help you deal with this problem you've created. Don't thank me; it's my job.

So, if you can, try to visualize him disappearing, winking out, the way the picture on the television used to become a white dot in the middle of the screen before it vanished. Close the eyes inside your head, the ones you are using to see the corridor and the elevator and the man, and concentrate hard. Be warned that it is easier to imagine something into being than it is to make it go away, particularly if it is something unpleasant that you don't want to think about. Unwanted, looming things have a tendency to hang around more insistently the more you try to get rid of them. So don't be disappointed if you open your eyes again (inside your head) and find that he's still there.

Open one of your mind's eyes cautiously. Is he gone? He is? Thank god for that. Now we can get back on track and work on relaxing without such a powerful distraction.

Finally you feel the elevator come to rest. After a moment, the doors are going to slide open and you will look outside. But before they do that, wait a moment. Don't let the doors open yet. Listen to me first. Only if you want to of course, nothing is mandatory. But this is important and if you've bothered to come this far, you might as well hear what I have to say, don't you think? Because I want to warn you about something.

Beyond the open elevator doors is the place that you have been longing to go but didn't even know it. What is it like? I can't tell you that. It is whatever place makes you feel like you belong there. That will be different for each of you. Once I tried this exercise with a man who, when the doors opened, saw his own office with its desk and chair and telephone. He was a lawyer and it turned out that what he really liked most in the world was to be at work, with the clock of his billable hours ticking by nicely while he prepared divorce papers or personal injury suits or last wills and testaments. At home, with his beautiful wife and three small children, he was always slightly on edge; he felt like he was an actor playing a father and flubbing almost half his lines and most of his entrances and exits. He would come into his office on Monday and experience a great surge of relief, but it was not until he opened those elevator doors and saw his favorite place—as he had always in his heart of hearts known it to be—that he could admit this to himself. He was happier after that; it changed his life but only because he was honest.

What I'm telling you is this, and I hope you'll listen to me because I am after all the one guiding this meditation: be honest. It might be that your favorite place is a lovely, bosky forest glen with the smell of pine trees and a crystal-clear blue lake beyond with a waterfall emptying into it in the distance, blah, blah, blah. There might be deer grazing amid the shafts of sunlight and a breeze ruffling the leaves. But really, the number of times I've gone around the "sharing circle" after a class and someone has talked about a place just like that, or about being on a beach with golden sand, or about a garden full of blooming flowers like one they saw when they were a child, well, please: if I got paid for each time that occurred, I would not have bothered to make this recording because I'd be too busy shopping. And for at least half of those people, I knew that they were not telling the truth, that they were telling me about a place they thought they were supposed to like, what they'd seen in advertisements on television. Not the place that really, deep down in their hearts, they truly longed for.

You can make up something like that if you want. There's nothing I can do to stop you because it's your mind and your desire and only you can know if you have really told yourself the truth. You may not even know you are lying to yourself when you look out of those elevator doors and see a Disney-style castle with white spires and banners waving and liveried footmen and a red carpet leading you inside. Or a boat the shape of a swan filled with silken cushions and all the chocolate you can eat. You might really believe that is the place you long to be. And perhaps you will be right. But I don't think so.

It is much more likely that the place you really want to be above all others is not like that at all. It is likely to be a place that no one else could possibly guess, that other people may not find beautiful or even remotely appealing. To give you an example: my place is a supermarket parking lot. There, I've told you. When I was a child, my mother always bought me an ice-cream cone after she was finished with the groceries, and when I think about my happiest memories, they are of walking across the asphalt to the car after my mother and her rattling cart, taking the first cold bite. It meant that all was right with the world and that week my father wouldn't open the cupboard door in the kitchen and say, "Why the hell isn't there any food in this house?" and my mother wouldn't throw something or storm upstairs to cry. When I think about that parking lot I feel one thing: safe. And for that reason it is beautiful to me, the way the parking spaces make their golden grid on the black asphalt, the way the cars slide in and out of their spaces fitting in like pieces in a jigsaw puzzle, like they were meant to be there.

So now you know. That's all I have to say. You can go ahead, when you are ready, and let the doors slide open. Look at what is outside. Step through the doors. Walk forward and explore this place that you have come so far to find. Look around and listen and touch things and, above all, do not be afraid.

Oh, one more thing. There may be some of you who, when you tried to make the weird man inside the elevator disappear, did not succeed. When you looked again, he was still there, waiting in the corner, not speaking, looking at his shoes, which you had just noticed were unnaturally large even for so tall a person. The shoes were thick-soled and looked like they might have steel toes. Also, there was a bit of spittle at the corner of his mouth, whitish and congealed. This unnerved you even more and you felt your heart beating and you could not wait for the elevator doors to open so you could get out of there and run away from this weird, rumbling, ugly creature.

As I said before, I don't know what you should do about the man. Now that the elevator doors are open, you could, as you planned, run away from him, into the place you've dreamed up and perhaps you'll lose him among the giant ferns or bookshelves or whatever might be out there. But you might not. He could come after you and find you. He might be able to run fast in spite of all appearances to the contrary.

So I suggest that you don't run away. I don't think you have too many other options at this point. If you can't make him vanish from a fantasy that you yourself created, then there is really only one thing left for you to do. Obviously, you don't have to follow my advice; you are in charge, you are the one that this is all about, the important one, the person that we are doing all of this to try to help. This is only a suggestion, nothing more.

Turn to face the weird man in the corner. Try looking

at his face if you can stand it. Then try holding out your hand to him. Open, palm up. Go on. He might take it in his own hand, which turns out to be enormous, oddly shaped, maybe with the wrong number of fingers, but warm and dry and strangely comforting. Then, without letting go, try stepping forward, leading him gently out of that back corner of the elevator into the light and space. What does he do? Will he follow?

Good. See, he's not so terrifying after all, just ugly and a little sad. But even though he's not the companion you might aspire to have, he's the one you created for yourself, so don't let go of his hand. Keep leading him forward. Now you are not alone anymore. Now you have a friend. Now you can go out and look around together.

Viral

None of the parents had any idea what was coming. All of them said the same thing. Sondra Patel from Boston told me: *He was not an unhappy boy as far as I could tell. He played soccer on the school team. He had friends. And he was a DJ, too, you know. People came to hear him play.*

Lorraine and Kenneth Mueller from Burke, Virginia, insisted that their daughter Kelly had not been depressed. *We had her tested many times,* Mrs. Mueller told me. *We kept an eye on her. Any sign of something wrong or different, we'd make sure that she went to a psychiatrist right away.* Mr. Mueller added: *That's right. We had her thoroughly checked out. Not one of them ever told us there was anything wrong with her. In fact, a couple of them told us we should stop bringing her in at all.*

One man even suggested that we should consider seeing a counselor ourselves, if you can believe that, Mrs. Mueller said. She snorted at the absurdity of it. Then she began to cry.

Sarah Weinberg and Clifford Jackson from Brooklyn, New York, held a photo of their son Damian up for me to see. In the picture he was grinning broadly, proudly showing the camera a new electric guitar and making a peace sign with this left hand. *A birthday present?* I asked; Ms. Weinberg nodded. She looked around the room at the other parents.

I don't know, she said. *I don't feel like we have anything in common with these other people. We're not really part of the mainstream of American culture and we don't buy into its capitalist consumerist ideals. Of course, there are stresses associated with being a biracial family but we were conscientious about discussing those openly with Damian, helping him to process his experiences. I just keep asking: why us?*

Although most of the conference attendees were Americans, there were some parents who had made the trip from abroad: a couple from London, another from Istanbul. Some Australians and some Germans. A Japanese man told me through a translator that when he went into his daughter's bedroom to wake her for school in the morning and found her gone, his heart plunged into his stomach. *My life ended that day,* he said.

I told him, as I'd told the others, how sorry I was for his loss. He nodded and said something to the translator. *What about you? Why are you here?* the translator relayed. I told him

I was covering the conference for a newspaper and showed him my press card. He looked at me, doubtfully. *Is that all?*

Well, I said, *I had a niece . . . Her mother isn't here.*

Ahh, so desu . . . he said. He nodded again, like I'd confirmed something he'd guessed already.

The story was the same all over the big, brightly lit, fabric-lined hotel ballroom. All the men and women who were attending the conference told me in their own way that they had been caught completely by surprise by what had happened to their children. By what their children had done.

They insisted that they were good people, that they were or (here several of them corrected themselves, sadly) *had been* good parents. They'd tried their best to be vigilant against threats to their children's well-being. They had warned them about strangers and predators and drug pushers. They had encouraged regular exercise. They had been attentive to signs of unchecked mental distress. They had kept up on the latest dangers that loomed up, out there, in the world ready to blight and blast young lives before they had a chance to grow. . . . Mrs. Mueller began to hyperventilate and had to be escorted from the room by her husband. They had done their best.

They were victims themselves as much as their children had been.

Who in your opinion were the perpetrators? I asked. Several of them looked at me aghast and wouldn't speak to me again.

This was the end of a long day that had begun in the morning with a plenary session addressed by Ms. Carolyn Williams, the driving force behind organizing the conference. She told the assembled attendees that bringing them all together had brought her life meaning after the terrible events of May 17th and that she hoped and prayed that they would find solace in one another's company, that they would cry together and heal together. That they would find hope to begin to rebuild their lives. Tears streamed down her face.

After that there were break-out groups, then lunch, then a series of panels of people from various disciplines—psychology, sociology, communications, technology—who had studied the phenomenon of 5/17 and tried to illuminate the reasons for its occurrence or to develop reliable methods for preventing something like it happening in the future. The session that I attended was chaired by a psychoanalyst who claimed that the problem was that this generation of children had been raised to view their lives as renewable; cyberspace had fundamentally confused the development of the self-protective ego instincts. The children believed they could simply restart the game when it was over, and so the concept of death had become abstracted to them, vacant; it had ceased to have any sense of gravity.

A man stood up in the back row.

Are you telling me that I raised a son who didn't know the difference between a video game and reality?

Perhaps not consciously, the psychoanalyst replied. *But, yes, somewhere deep in his unconscious, there was a flaw, a fatal error, buried and forgotten, waiting to explode . . .*

Bullshit, said the father in the back row and left the room letting the door slam behind him.

There seemed to be similar disgruntlement with the

other professionals who spoke. I passed a group of mothers who were all talking angrily about a social psychologist who had told them that the problem was the isolation in which people now lived. The anxiety of parents about their children's safety had caused them to curtail the freedom of their children to roam and to have "unstructured" time. As a result, the only genuine playing that these kids did was online, where they built extensive and elaborate networks of trust and interaction stretching far beyond the boundaries of their physical communities. These kids had been conclusively demonstrated to feel pressure to conform and to gain the respect of their peer group, as they did in conventional "real world" peer groups. But the rules for how to do this were different in these widely dispersed networks and worked on a consumerist model—the only model these kids were familiar with. Since the usual measures of social value in American society (wealth, beauty) were stripped away by the medium, the only thing left by which children could measure success or failure was simple: quantity.

So they felt that they had to have more friends than anyone else; and then they needed to show that these weren't just names on a list but real, genuine bonds, people whom they trusted and who trusted them back. People to whom they were connected in some deep and ineradicable way. What could they do to demonstrate this bond? Well, the evidence was before us all . . .

The mothers were outraged. They absolutely rejected the man's explanation of their children's deaths. He was disrespectful, unfeeling, a crank, a charlatan.

It occurred to me that, really, people didn't want an

explanation of what had happened. They wanted it to remain a mystery now and forever. This was understandable. Any theory that thoroughly and adequately accounted for the May 17th Fires, as they were known in the press coverage afterward, would reduce all these people's particular children, whom they had loved and cherished as unique, to something standardized, identical, the same. It would erase the individuality of each child, which was all they had left now: the way, for example, Annabel, my niece, loved the word "exceedingly" when she was a child, how she pronounced it as if there were four e's in it—*exceeeedingly*. Or how she used to show me her gymnastics every time I visited. Or how she used to climb up the tree in her backyard and hide among the branches until someone came to find her. That was before she turned into an almost-teenager who spent all her time in front of the computer in her room.

Any wholesale explanation for 5/17 would mean that, as far as it affected the most important matter of their young lives, all these different children might as well have been the same child, raised by the same parents. No one wanted to accept that.

This was why, I think, the conference fell apart at the end of that first day. The chaos broke out when the poet Lisa Romini-Malone got up to read the long poem she had composed for the occasion. She was not herself a Parent of 5/17 but, she said, she had close friends among those who'd lost their bright hopes for the future and she felt she could channel some of their pain through the profound act of empathy that was writing.

The parents sat attentive. Ms. Romini-Malone began to

read. I think it was at the line: *Burning forth in a magnificent fire / Their young and precious hearts* that the trouble began. Or it might have been when she said: *Planning in secret / The message passed from hand to hand like signal fires.* There was a murmuring in the hall that grew until it began to drown out the speaker at the front. Ms. Williams stood up and asked the audience for quiet. A woman called out from the third row: *She's celebrating this, like it is something great that happened! Like it was something beautiful,* and after that there was no quieting the room. What the poet said was lost in the angry, undifferentiated roar that came from the until-then polite and contained audience. It was a sound like the ocean rising up in a storm to burst over the land, unreasonable, unreasoning and bottomless: the sound of grief. As if united into one force, the parents rushed toward the podium and toppled it and then kept going, out into the carpeted halls of the hotel, knocking over ficus plants and tables, smashing lamps, tearing the deliberately inoffensive art down from the walls.

I stayed sheltered in a recessed window of the room with some other journalists until the main energy of the riot had made its way out into the corridor and the main lobby downstairs. Then I followed at a distance, watching from the mezzanine balcony and taking notes for the story I would write and file later that evening. Soon, from outside in the street, there came the undulating sound of sirens as the police pulled up in front of the hotel.

As I watched them storm in through the doors and push the mass of rioting parents back with their big, Plexiglas shields, I remembered, suddenly and vividly, the May morning, almost two years earlier, when the telephone woke me with its bleating and it was my sister on the other end screaming how something had happened to her daughter. I remembered how I turned on the television to the news and saw those first, terrible images that everyone knows now so well.

And I remembered how a few months earlier than that, when my sister was concerned that Annabel was spending so much time with her computer instead of with her friends, I told her not to worry. Annabel was just shy like I had been at her age, she would grow out of it, she would be fine, I said. *You have a tendency to over-parent just like Mom*, I said, feeling pleased with myself for speaking plainly to my older sister, standing up to her. *Leave Annabel alone. She'll be okay.*

Then May 17th arrived. All across the world, children executed what they'd organized in secret, never speaking of their plan out loud and communicating only with a network of others whom they knew just as words and images onscreen, by email, on discussion boards, through cell phones, in coded messages and downloaded, encrypted files, so that just before 11 p.m. EST, they left their homes and climbed whatever they could find that was tall enough, carrying those useless homemade parachutes that one of them, no one would ever know who, had designed.

Some climbed water towers; others went onto the roofs of houses or apartment buildings. One boy in Tucson climbed up the inside of the enormous tilted dish of a radio telescope. A girl in San Francisco pulled herself onto the railings of the Golden Gate Bridge. They took their places in the dark. They waited for the hour to arrive. And when it did, they lit the fireworks they'd tied onto their ankles or wrists or stuffed into their backpacks and launched themselves out so that they all blazed up in a single moment and then plummeted burning through the night engulfed by flames before they hit the ground and burned and guttered there like candles laid out in remembrance of something, then forgotten.

Down in the lobby, the police were starting to cuff and take away the rioters, though some were still breaking and dismantling the furnishings. Below me a woman was sitting on the floor, holding her head, looking dazed. A man, perhaps her husband, tried to comfort her. I thought about my niece, how on earth it might have been for her as she fell from the eighth floor of the library in town—to which she had the key because she volunteered there twice a week—how she must have known at some point that the parachute was not going to save her and how entirely alone she must have been. I felt something like a wave of molten lava rising up inside my body and I tried to tamp it down as I had done many times before, keeping a careful hold of myself so that I could report objectively on all that had occurred. But I did not succeed this time, and the great, hot mass welled up out of my chest and came out of my mouth as a sound I'd never heard myself or anyone else make until that moment and before I knew what I was doing, I found that I was running down the wide, carpeted staircase, with my fists swinging out in front of me, still shouting without words and looking, looking, looking for something, anything to smash.

Biographies

I.

Emily Mitchell was born in London in the middle of a garbage collectors' strike. The strike began when the year had just crawled out from winter and it was still cold and rainy and the garbage collectors were unhappy because exponential growth in the manufacture and use of disposable food containers had added to their workload but there had been no expanded hiring to meet this increased demand. The leader of their union was a charismatic man called Donkey who got his moniker for his very long ears and braying voice as well as for his stubborn nature, although it is worth noting that Donkey, whose real name was Clive, was also a father and husband whose wife and children remember him as very kind, gentle and patient.

All spring the garbage piled up against the walls of the city. Fruit and scraps of meat dampened and drooped; vegetables blackened, frayed, disintegrated. Bristling animals slipped in and out of the mounting piles of plastic bags and bottles, beverage cartons, tin cans, old shoes. Children had to be warned not to play and climb on the heaps of refuse clogging up the streets, but some nevertheless made games of running up their sides and some of them fell into the piles of trash and had to be rescued. In places around town, whole streets were blocked and traffic had to be diverted.

In the end, the government decided to settle with the garbage collectors, but by this time the mountains of trash were so high and so dense from the pressures of the layers above that they could not be moved by the normal means. In some places the city used helicopters to dislodge the mass of compacted matter and hoist it into the air so that it could be flown away. People who were alive at that time remember from that summer the frequent spectacle of fleets of helicopters flying across the sky, each with a misshapen mass attached beneath it on the end of a long cord, silhouetted against the setting sun. As picturesque as these flights were, they had the disadvantage that the masses of garbage would lose their integrity in flight and start to shed, showering the populace below with banana peels and old chocolate-bar wrappers.

By the time Emily Mitchell was born, in the fall of that year, most of the garbage had been cleared away. Some of it had been buried and the land above turned into parks. Some of it had been moved to a secret location. The strike was over and the growling trucks moved again through the blue early streets waking people before dawn.

One surprising after effect of the strike was not discovered until the following year. It was found that several species of insects, including a variety of butterfly, and some types of flowering plants—a ragweed, a tasslewort—had begun to adapt to the garbage mountains even in the short time they existed. These insects and plants had changed their colors and in some cases their shapes in order to camouflage themselves more effectively and had come to mimic the prevalent designs found in their new environment. The bold red-and-white design of the Coca-Cola can in particular seems to have inspired these adaptations, and several of the plants began to select for a mutation of brilliant scarlet with white curlicues. Even today, these flowers can be seen growing wild in unexpected places around the city. They are deemed rare and desirable and expensive—when they can be found. Efforts to raise them commercially have not been successful. So if you can locate them, you can sell them for a remarkable sum.

2.

Emily Mitchell has worked as a waitress, a receptionist at a bakery/tanning salon, a short-order cook, a snowmobile driver, a crime-scene cleanup technician, an exotic animal trainer, a war correspondent, a phone dispatcher, a secretary, an environmental campaigner, a freelance journalist, a bean counter and a holistic pediatric oncologist.

She has never worked as an exotic dancer. She might have done this—since she has no moral objection to sex work as such and certainly not to the deliberate and conscious choice by women to use their sexual desirability, long the source of their unjust and egregious oppression, as a means of obtaining economic and social power—if only her breasts had been bigger. Not *much* bigger, but big enough that they appeared large in proportion to her torso, which seems to be the important ratio in these cases. Or maybe it was her torso that was too big. Or her hips, which are round and scoop-shaped, so her body is like a tulip bulb or an old-fashioned earthenware jug. She thinks she might have been pretty good at exotic dancing, actually, if not for her overwhelming self-consciousness, her basic discomfort with disrobing in front of people with whom she's not intimate, her physical clumsiness and her inconvenient but persistent sense that there is something exploitative about the whole endeavor.

She obtained a joint degree in neuroscience and engineering from the American University of Southern Abkhazia and a master of fine arts from the Iowa Writers' Workshop. She taught English in Japan for several years but was fired when it was discovered that she had been deliberately teaching her students a dialect entirely of her own invention because she thought it would be "amusing" to create a group of people who spoke a wholly imaginary language without being aware of it. She said, in a statement at the time of her termination: "I wanted to make something beautiful and aloof, a language that floated in the world with the levitating detachment of a cumulus cloud. I had only the best intentions and I am sorry for anyone whom I have hurt." At the end of her statement she added several sentences in her invented language, which no one except one or two of her more advanced students understood and which they would not translate when asked for comment. After that she was led away and deported.

3.

Emily Mitchell's first novel *The Art Historian's Daughter-in-Law* was published in 2009 and was almost entirely plagiarized from the work of the nineteenth-century Norwegian novelist Amund Eilertsen. She was immediately sued by the Eilertsen estate for copyright infringement but argued successfully that, because she stole material from more than one of Eilersten's novels, her book constituted an entirely new work of literature that crucially reframed and reimagined the content of the original and therefore was a legitimate contribution to the intellectual conversation of our time. She is now working on a novel that combines excerpts from the works of George Eliot with lyrics by the Rolling Stones.

Her short fiction has appeared in various publications and then disappeared. This is unusual and seems to be attributable to a peculiar warp in the space-time continuum, which her work has caught like a virus and which makes it vanish shortly after publication never to be seen again. There were recently rumors that some of her stories had inexplicably turned up in a computer seized by police in Harare, Zimbabwe, but these are uncorroborated and may in fact have been a hoax perpetrated to generate publicity for her forthcoming novel.

4.

Emily Mitchell lives in Cleveland, Ohio, or at least she is fairly certain that is where she lives. Some mornings she wakes up and isn't sure. She looks out the window and the street seems different: it looks more like a street near the Bund in Shanghai, flanked by heavy Victorian hotels, crowded with bicycles and loud with car horns. Or one of the precipitous canyons in midtown Manhattan, which are perfectly designed for all kinds of animals, like peregrine falcons, rats, mice and cockroaches and for the significant percentage of people who dream at night that they can grow a reflective shell over their skin, become dark and shiny as an automobile and move through the world smoothly as if they were being drawn forward on a thread. Emily Mitchell is not one of these people.

Mostly, however, she gets up and looks outside and sees the old, once-grand houses and the tossing deciduous trees of northeastern Ohio and she is quite pleased.

What does it really mean to "live" in a place anyway? There have been some places where she's resided for even years at a time that so flattened and enervated her that she felt like she barely existed, a sketch of a woman, a leaf skeleton with a smile that she pulled open like the tray on the back of an airplane seat. There have been other places that made her so dizzy she could hardly stand or places in which she felt like she was falling, hurtling downward at a steady, terminal velocity, flailing to grab hold of something that could stop her, a ledge of some kind, but was never quite able to lay hold of anything to stop her plunge.

Can this really be described as "living" in the sense we usually mean?

She tries to avoid these places when she can. Someday she wants to go back and understand the nature of their poison, maybe dig a garden there. But for the moment she is content where she is.

Cleveland is not as crowded with stories that have already been told as the great cities of the US coasts or Europe, or as those places like Gettysburg or Selma or Hiroshima where history pivoted in ways that are very clear. For this reason you must peer at Cleveland a little harder to see it. Although it has since fallen on hard times, it was once a place of great, ostentatious wealth, the home and resting place of John D. Rockefeller. In those robber-baron days, so different from our own time, there was little restriction on what the rich could do with their money, and they lived in a world made of mirrors in which even their friends merely served to reflect back at them their sense of their own virtue and importance.

It is a less-known fact about Rockefeller that he loved to disguise himself as a working man and go into his own businesses and factories in order to see without being seen the running of his enterprises. One day when he had just started working in one of his refineries, he was ordered by the foreman to replace the man who oversaw the furnace that heated the oil before distilling, in spite of the fact that he had no experience at this work and no skill at it. When Rockefeller refused, the foreman threatened him with violence if he didn't comply, saying that the furnace must be kept running at all costs to meet the quota set for the factory or they would all lose their jobs. Rockefeller then removed his disguise and revealed his identity, telling the foreman who he really was. But in those days before television, people did not necessarily recognize the faces of even the most prominent citizens and the foreman just looked at him and laughed.

"Sure you're Rockefeller," he is said to have replied, "and I'm Queen Victoria. Now get over to that furnace and get working."

It is not clear whether the accident that occurred that day can be attributed to Rockefeller's inexperience and incompetence because little is known about its details. It is the nature of explosions to erase the evidence of their own causes. It was close to midday. There was a sudden flower of fire and a roar and the furnace showered jots of liquid metal from its mouth that sewed flames wherever they landed. Fourteen men were killed including the newly hired man, whose name no one could quite remember—James or Jed or something like that—who was consumed so completely by the fire that afterward no one could recognize his face. It was only when Rockefeller's personal secretary, hearing the news, raced down to the factory and made inquiries that the body was identified by the rings the man wore which, although they were disfigured by the heat, were still attached to the dead man's hands.

Rockefeller is buried beneath a giant obelisk in a cemetery on the heights overlooking the city. From that spot you can see over the roofs of the houses where the millionaires used to live, to the places where the factories used to be, to where the workers used to live in crowded row houses, all the way down to the shores of the lake that used to carry boats that took the goods made there all around the country and the world. On a clear day, it is a wonderful view.

5.

Emily Mitchell lives with her husband, whom she sometimes loves so much that she'd like to climb inside his chest and stay there, curled up like a cat. She likes to lie against him so it feels as if their ribs have become clasped like fingers and when they try to get up they will have trouble pulling them apart. She couldn't say exactly why she feels this way and she is frequently surprised by the persistence of this feeling over so many years. Her husband is often charming, smart and considerate. But he can also be melancholy and cantankerous from time to time. He has been known on occasion to worry too much about something that really wasn't so terrible after all.

Nevertheless, she seems always to come back to her underlying enduring affection for him. Since they are both writers, they have moved around a lot and they don't own very much material stuff like furniture or durable goods or electronics. Sometimes Emily Mitchell finds this frustrating. She will look at the empty rooms in her house and imagine all the things that could go in them. Wouldn't it be nice to have an Empire chair in that corner? Wouldn't a Danish modern coffee table be just the thing in the living room? She longs to own furnishings for which she knows only the names and not the functions, like an armoire or a credenza, an ottoman, a secretary or a chifferobe. But then she wonders whether all these things would look good together and she thinks that perhaps it is better to imagine them than to have them, so that other people can't see how badly they clash and judge her for having bad taste or lacking any sense of design. Her husband doesn't care much about furniture or the names of furniture.

For a while a few years ago, Emily Mitchell and her husband lived apart because they had jobs in different cities. They would call each other every night on the phone.

"Hello?"

"Hello!"

"He-llo . . ."

"*Hello*."

In the background of these calls, they could sometimes hear the weather where the other one was. Sometimes Emily Mitchell could hear a police car drive past her husband's apartment with its siren blaring or a bus rumble or a rainstorm begin. On the phone, heavy rain sounded like hot oil crackling in a pan. Sometimes they would leave their phones on after they had nothing left to say so that they could hear each other turn the pages of their books while they read themselves to sleep. The turning pages sounded louder on the phone than they would have if they had been lying side by side; in fact, it sounded like they were each reading a giant book, maybe about the size of a bed, with huge, heavy pages. Emily Mitchell would listen to the sound of her husband turning the pages of his giant book. Eventually the sound would make her sleepy; she would relax listening for the next page to turn. She would feel less lonely and more comfortable until at last she could put her head down and go to sleep.

Acknowledgments

These stories are the work of many years and I had a lot of help with them, for which I am extremely grateful. Stephen Donadio and Carolyn Kuebler gave me invaluable, deeply appreciated support and encouragement; Meakin Armstrong, Terrance Hayes, Ronald Spatz and Chris Beha were thoughtful editors. I owe a great debt to Gail Hochman, my amazing agent. Jill Bialosky, my editor, chose, championed, shaped, and guided this book brilliantly through the editorial process; her assistant Angie Shih was smart and helpful; Nancy Palmquist did wonderful editing work, insightful and precise, on the manuscript.

Maud Casey, Howard Norman, Stanley Plumly and all my colleagues at the University of Maryland have welcomed and inspired me, as my colleagues at Cleveland State University, most especially Michael Dumanis and Imad Rahman, did before. A CAPAA grant from the Graduate School of the University of Maryland and a fellowship from Virginia Center for the Creative Arts gave me time to write. As always, my family has been generous and kind and they have never once told me I really should think about doing something more sensible with my life than writing made-up stories. My dad got me hooked on science fiction early and my mom made sure that I eventually read other things as well. Joanna Mitchell gives me light and courage. Joshua Tyree remains the writer I admire most and my very favorite, much beloved husband.